What the critics are saying...

ଽଠ

"The decadent surroundings coupled with Maddie and Ash's erotic encounters make for a very sensual tale. There are also touches of humor and sweetness that lighten the story, creating a wonderful blend of lust and love." ~ *Romance Reviews Today*

"Erotic and adventurous, this book will heat up any reader's day and have them wishing for their own personal vacation." ~ *The Romance Studio*

"...with Jessica Darian's direct and engaging style Hedonist's Paradise is a sexy love story that's exciting and uplifting." ~ *Just Erotic Romance Reviews*

Jessica Darian

Hedonist's PARADISE

ELLORA'S CAVE
ROMANTICA PUBLISHING

An Ellora's Cave Romantica Publication

www.ellorascave.com

Hedonist's Paradise

ISBN 1419953478
ALL RIGHTS RESERVED.
Hedonist's Paradise Copyright © 2005 Jessica Darian
Edited by Kelli Kwiatkowski.
Cover art by Syneca.

Electronic book Publication July 2005
Trade paperback Publication July 2006

Warning:

The following material contains graphic sexual content meant for mature readers. This story has been rated S-*ensuous* by a minimum of three independent reviewers.

Ellora's Cave Publishing offers three levels of Romantica™ reading entertainment: S (S-ensuous), E (E-rotic), and X (X-treme).

S-*ensuous* love scenes are explicit and leave nothing to the imagination.

E-*rotic* love scenes are explicit, leave nothing to the imagination, and are high in volume per the overall word count. In addition, some E-rated titles might contain fantasy material that some readers find objectionable, such as bondage, submission, same sex encounters, forced seductions, and so forth. E-rated titles are the most graphic titles we carry; it is common, for instance, for an author to use words such as "fucking", "cock", "pussy", and such within their work of literature.

X-*treme* titles differ from E-rated titles only in plot premise and storyline execution. Unlike E-rated titles, stories designated with the letter X tend to contain controversial subject matter not for the faint of heart.

Also by Jessica Darian

ઔ

The Panty Episode

About the Author

ઔ

Jessica lives in the Pacific Northwest with her husband and two young children. Time is a precious commodity in her house, so she uses it wisely—reading and writing as much as she can! On the rare occasion she has time to spare, she whips up new recipes in the kitchen, adds to her gemstone collection or moves through a few Sun Salutations. She loves to chat with readers, so please feel free to send her an email!

Jessica welcomes comments from readers. You can find her website and email address on her author bio page at www.ellorascave.com.

HEDONIST'S PARADISE

৯০

Dedication

ଋଚ

To my grandmother Marilyn and my husband Travis.
Your support and inspiration have meant the world to me.
This one's for you.

Trademarks Acknowledgement

The author acknowledges the trademarked status and trademark owners of the following wordmarks mentioned in this work of fiction:

Chippendales: Chippendales USA
GQ: Advance Magazine Publishers Inc.
Jell-O: Kraft Foods Holdings, Inc.
Kama Sutra: Kamsut, Inc.
Palm Pilot: Pirani, Amin
Ronald McDonald: McDonald's Corporation

Chapter One

❧

"Maddie, come on! Could you think of a more perfect place to spend a vacation?"

Madison Summers eyed the glossy brochure being waved under her nose with resignation. It wasn't the first time her best friend had tried to talk her into something like this. Unfortunately, it also wouldn't be the last.

"Well, I can't see it if you won't hold still," she grumbled, trying to snatch the brochure before it could smack her in the face again.

Before she could grab it, Kris swept it behind her back. "Wait just a second. As your friendly neighborhood travel agent, it's my job to find your dream destination." She tapped the brochure and smiled at Maddie. "This is exactly where you need to be."

"Kris, I really don't think a luxury spa and resort is my sort of place."

Kris graced her with an exaggerated eye roll. "Here we go. Okay, let's hear it. Tell me all of the reasons why Maddie Summers can't go. Why it won't work. Why you can't spend the money. Blah, blah, blah…"

With a wave of her hand, Maddie replied, "You can imagine what sort of people frequent a place like that. Rich, snobby and perfect in their little spa robes and —"

Kris snorted. "So? What do you care what everybody looks and acts like? You don't have to socialize. You can stay in your room and drink martinis naked. That's part of the beauty of this place."

"Second," Maddie continued, as if Kris hadn't spoken, "there's the cost. You actually think I would pay thousands of dollars just to have someone paint my toes and massage my back? I know you said for a luxury spa and resort, that's a great price for what it includes, but my god! I could stay home with a stack of books and a few pints of ice cream and have just as much fun for less than sixty bucks."

"Yeah, and if you did that you'd gain ten pounds and become a hermit. You know you can easily afford this place. You've worked your butt off for the past few years and saved every penny. Don't you think you deserve to play a little now?"

"By drinking in my room naked? And alone?"

"Hon, the alone part would be optional, trust me." Kris flashed a wicked grin at her.

Confused, Maddie asked, "What does that mean?" A horrible thought entered her mind. "What a minute. This isn't one of those places where desperate women go and pay the cabana boys to sleep with them, is it?"

"No! You think I would send you to a place like that?" Kris laughed. "You're thinking of the cruise ships. Besides, what if you found a really *hot* cabana boy?"

Maddie searched her friend's face. Had her laugh been a little forced? Why was her gaze so innocent when Kris was usually anything but? Highly suspicious, she asked, "What is this all about, really?"

Kris shook her head in pity. "Hon, when was the last time you took a vacation?"

"Well, it's been awhile, but—"

"No, it's been longer than awhile," Kris interrupted.

Maddie nodded, unable to argue. "You're right. It has been a long time, but so what?"

"So what?" Two blonde eyebrows shot up. "You know what they say about all work and no play, don't you? You miss out on all the gorgeous men who want to—"

Maddie groaned loudly, cutting off whatever Kris might have said next. Her friend was known to enjoy life to the fullest. Including every attractive man who caught her eye.

"No, seriously. A woman needs a little fun now and then. You haven't taken the time to stop and smell the roses for a long time. Don't you wonder what you've been missing?"

A negligent shrug was Maddie's only answer. She could see her friend's point, but it wasn't enough to justify such a large expense. Not to mention the fact they were talking about a place where she would be so far out of her element it was a sure bet for disaster.

"Okay," Kris sighed. "Let's go at this from a different angle. Is it the money?"

"That's part of it."

"Why?" Kris countered relentlessly. "We both know you can afford it. Think about it. If you can't spend your hard-earned money on yourself, who will you spend it on?"

"True," she conceded. "But why can't it be somewhere a little more practical?"

Now it was her friend's turn to groan. "Oh, come on. The whole point of a spa is to be a little *impractical*. To treat yourself to a well-earned week of bliss."

Bliss? Put like that, Maddie had to admit it sounded a little bit fun. The small chink in her resolve was slowly growing larger. But true to her nature, she valiantly tried to gain a foothold. "Kris, I'm not the kind of person who blows money on a place like that. I spent quite a bit of my savings on my house. So my penny supply is considerably depleted."

"Maddie, money isn't an issue. We both know that."

Maddie stared at the glass of iced tea in her hand. Kris was right. She'd saved quite a bit and could easily afford this vacation. But there were also the various "what-ifs" that kept her from saying yes. What if she was fired? What if a friend needed help? What if her car died tomorrow and she needed a new one? Parting with so much money for one brief week of things she could easily do without just wasn't her style. But even that wasn't the whole truth.

Laying her head back against the sofa, she quietly admitted, "It's just not me. I'm not the type of person who flits away to a spa for a week to be shamelessly pampered. I could think of one hundred and one other things to do with my time and money. Useful things. Like my store."

"Hon, you need this. The store will open and you know it. No one deserves this vacation more than you do. Believe me." Normally dramatic, Kris stressed that last statement.

Setting her glass on the coffee table, Maddie rubbed her hands across her face as if to wipe away her doubts. "I know. God, I know. But what if something happens?"

Kris rolled her eyes and asked, "Like what? You can't let all the what-ifs stop you from—" Kris stopped and shook her head. "Look. You need a vacation. When was the last time you spent time or money on yourself?"

Maddie raised her defiant gaze to her friend's. "We just went through this. I've been working hard to—"

Kris cut her off impatiently, "Exactly. You've worked hard. Too hard. And now you need to treat yourself. You've more than proved your financial savvy, now it's time for you to reap the rewards by taking a vacation. It's time for you to live a little, Maddie."

Maddie chewed on her lower lip as her indecision warred with a tiny spark of excitement. Kris was right, and deep down she knew it.

But did she dare?

Could she really spend money—her hard-earned money—on an extravagant week of pure luxury? It had been a long while since she'd done anything for herself. If she didn't count her house. A girl needed to live somewhere, however. The small house she'd purchased boasted nothing more than two bedrooms and one bathroom. Her mortgage payments weren't much more than she'd pay for rent on an apartment.

But this vacation?

This was so much more than splurging on a box of imported chocolates. Or spending three hundred dollars on a pair of shoes or a new handbag. She could go on and on. Of course, she hadn't splurged on any of those things. In fact, she had never spent money on any frivolous indulgence for herself. So maybe—just maybe—she was entitled to treat herself now.

As if sensing her uncertainty, Kris went in for the kill. "Believe me, this place has gotten rave reviews." Her smug smile gave Maddie a twinge of apprehension. "They have massages, facials, manicures and pedicures, to name a few. You can take yoga classes or aerobics. There are walking trails…oh, and you sleep in your own 'lavish bungalow'. They're arranged in clusters of five and the one you'll stay in surrounds a pleasure garden with a hot tub." She waggled her eyebrows at Maddie. "I wonder what sort of activities they have in the pleasure garden? Maybe the bungalows around you will be filled with gorgeous single men."

At her snort, Kris shrugged, the mischievous gleam still in her eyes. "Well, you never know. Anyway this place sounds like it will be paradise for you. I researched quite a few resorts before I found this one. Trust me, Maddie, once you get there, you'll see just how perfect it is for you. After reading about it, I'm even tempted to sneak in with your luggage."

Maddie didn't even try to suppress the small smile that curved her lips. Ever since Kris had started working for a travel agency, she'd tried to tempt Maddie into taking a vacation at a spa, a ski resort, a dude ranch, and a half dozen bed-and-breakfasts around the nation. Not to mention that new age resort that specialized in detoxifying your system with a week of juice-only diets, complete with a colon flush, or whatever they had called it. The idea of anyone trying to "flush" away the toxins in her body by those means had freaked her out.

Up until now she'd had no problem saying no. But with all the hours she'd been putting in recently at the office, along with the weekends spent getting her store ready, she was ready for some downtime. Not necessarily an expensive week at a spa, but somewhere she could relax. Of course, it didn't hurt that she could get a massage and a facial at this place. Or even sleep until lunchtime.

But still…could she really do it?

Kris threw up her hands as she watched the play of emotions on Maddie's face. "Fine, here it is. I dare you to go."

Maddie blinked. "You dare me?"

"Yep. I dare you to go on this vacation and have the time of your life. I know it's nice and comfortable in that little shell you've been living in, but you're missing way more of life than you should be. So go. Have a blast. Just grab life by the balls and give 'em a good twist." Using her hands, Kris demonstrated the best way to do just that.

Maddie couldn't help but feel the sting of those words. She'd been living in a shell? Well, she didn't go out much, but that was simply because she was a homebody. That didn't mean she lived in seclusion. Defensive now, she huffed, "You make it sound as if wanting a little downtime at home is a bad thing. I don't think you can compare being a homebody to living in a shell."

"You're not a homebody anymore Maddie, you're a recluse! You go to our yoga classes and that's the extent of your socializing. All I'm asking you to do is let go for a week and see what happens. Treat yourself. And if it's really as horrible as you're expecting, I'll never bother you about it again."

Maddie could feel herself weakening. A week of bliss did sound…refreshing. Something a little different. Something a little fun. However, it was more than that. This vacation was something she *should* do. For herself. And to prove to Kris she wasn't a recluse.

"Okay Kris, you win. Book me that bungalow with the pleasure garden," Maddie's voice was resigned, but she secretly felt almost good about her decision. A fact that surprised her.

Kris clapped her hands and practically crowed with delight. "Yes! I knew I'd wear you down eventually! You won't regret this."

Now it was Maddie's turn to roll her eyes. "Okay, okay. No gloating. What do I need to do to get the reservations?"

"Hon, that's what I'm here for, remember?" Her friend looked ready to get down to business. "Do you have your credit card with you?"

"Oh, sure. Let me grab it." Maddie wandered over to the table where she'd left her purse.

"Perfect. Grab everything and let's go." Kris was almost skipping toward the front door.

A sense of dread slowly came over Maddie. "Go where?"

The familiar glint in her friend's eyes nearly made her groan. "Shopping of course. You'll need new clothes and lingerie and at least two bikinis. And don't forget you'll need cute exercise clothes to attract any hotties that might be there."

She held up her hands as if to ward Kris off. "No, absolutely not. I agreed to go on vacation, not shop for new clothes I don't need."

"Maddie, have you looked in your closet lately?"

Rather than get defensive, Maddie shrugged her shoulders. "Just because you think my clothes are drab doesn't mean I need new ones."

Dragging her in front of the hallway mirror, Kris said, "Look at you. With your coloring, you could be wearing light shades that really flatter your complexion. Not to mention showing off a little cleavage and your long legs." Kris winked slyly. "Hon, if you've got it, flaunt it. And you've definitely got it. But instead, you only own clothes that are brown, gray or navy blue. All of which are varying shades of blah, in my book. And they definitely don't enhance what you've got. You need a few pieces that say *sex appeal*, not *what's sex*?"

The image reflected in the glass showed a woman with chestnut hair and hazel eyes. In her opinion, her lips were a little

Jessica Darian

too full and her skin was what poets would describe as porcelain. She'd always thought of it more as a pasty white. Going out in the sun was a guarantee for a painful burn.

Her five-foot-seven frame carried shapely curves that she had always thought could be a little less shapely. About fifteen pounds less shapely, to be exact. Maddie wasn't so critical she'd call herself ugly. Actually, she felt she was moderately attractive. She had simply never tried to do much with her appearance. It cost too much time, effort and, most importantly, money. Besides, when you were a single woman who rarely dated, what was the point?

She had always found a better use for her time than primping in front of a mirror. Of course, that didn't mean she hadn't ever wondered what the right shade of eye shadow and a sexy dress would do for her.

With a sigh, she knew she couldn't deny what Kris said. Catching her eye, Maddie replied firmly, "Nothing too frilly, too see-through, too revealing, or in any wild or funky colors. And no bikinis."

Wise enough to know she'd won a major battle, Kris hurried Maddie out the door and into her car before she could utter another word. Only after they were safely on their way did she dare to say, "Hon, you're going to look like a new woman when we're done."

Which was exactly what Maddie was afraid of.

"Oh, and Maddie?"

"Hmm?" Maddie was busy staring out the window, trying not to contemplate jumping as soon as the vehicle stopped.

"Everything is already booked and your flight leaves tomorrow at three." The words were spoken so quickly Maddie almost didn't catch them.

Horror slowly dawned.

She turned to look at Kris, certain she hadn't heard her right. But her best friend—make that ex-best friend—was

16

watching the road as if her life depended on it. If only she knew how much it did.

In a strangled voice, she croaked, "What. Did. You. Say?"

"Okay, I know I shouldn't have done that. But really, if I wouldn't have set it up, you and I both know you would have found a way to back out of this. Besides, you do need to get away and have some fun. I was only thinking of you." The last was said with an imploring look and innocent smile.

Maddie snorted in disgust. Though she didn't know if it was disgust with herself or Kris. Maybe a little of both. "You shouldn't have gone behind my back Kris."

"I'm really sorry." Though they both knew she wasn't. "You did agree to go, however. So what's the difference if it's tomorrow or two months from now?"

"Well, because…because there are things that need to be done," Maddie sputtered, as she grasped for excuses. "I have to ask for vacation days, find someone to get my mail, water my plants and all those other things," she finished lamely.

"Already taken care of. I talked to your boss a couple of weeks ago and she thought it was a great idea to surprise you with this vacation. And I'll take care of your mail, your plants and all those other things at home for you. You can leave me a list. Any other complaints?"

There had to be something. Her capitulation had been much too easy, she realized. Maddie searched her brain for any plausible excuse but came up empty-handed. "You've thought of everything, haven't you?" she muttered, but there was little heat to her words.

"I sure did. You just sit back and let me take care of the rest." Kris patted her leg in reassurance, though Maddie found little comfort in the gesture.

When she finally got home that evening, she could only collapse on her sofa with a heartfelt groan. Now she remembered why shopping with Kris was on her never-to-do list. The term "power shopping" didn't quite do justice to what she'd just experienced. Kris was a self-proclaimed shopaholic and had been in her element, while Maddie had prayed for oblivion after the first store.

She'd lost count of how many stores she'd been dragged through. Her arms had vehemently protested the mountain of bags she'd hauled around containing her purchases — each and every useless, frivolous one. Her credit card had almost melted under the pressure. With a grimace, she tried not to think about next month's bill.

Wait a minute.

To heck with the bill and her aching arms. Today wasn't about frivolous spending. It was about making choices and being responsible enough to deal with the consequences. Which she was. She'd pay that bill off next month and that'd be the end of it.

She was going to live a little, dammit.

With a weak smile of victory, she limped her way into the kitchen and pulled her favorite triple chocolate-fudge ice cream from the freezer. She knew she deserved it tonight.

* * * * *

The next morning Maddie woke up with an ice cream hangover. The sort that has a woman vowing never to touch the stuff again because her derriere has dropped, dimpled and otherwise expanded overnight. Ugh.

Sneaking a peek in the hallway mirror, she shuddered, wandering into the kitchen for coffee.

Her eyes were still bleary with sleep and her movements automatic as she measured the grounds. Maybe a strong pot would help to improve the mirror's image. If not, then it could be time to buy a new mirror.

As the aroma of her favorite fresh-brewed roast filled the air, she couldn't help but sigh with pleasure.

To heck with the mirror. She had a date with a big mug of java.

Two cups of coffee and a piece of toast later, Maddie felt much more human. It was a lazy Sunday morning and she was going to enjoy every minute of it.

As soon as that thought entered her mind, the phone started to ring. Tempted to ignore it, she heaved a big sigh, knowing she couldn't. The practical side of her always reasoned it could be someone with an emergency.

"Hello?"

"Maddie, have you started packing?"

She was more than a little surprised to hear Kris on the other end. Usually Kris was dead to the world until at least eleven on Sunday mornings. A glance at the clock told her it was only nine.

Maddie stared at the phone a second. "Um, packing?"

Her voice tinged with exasperation, Kris grumbled, "Yeah, packing. Or were you planning on going with only the clothes on your back? I'll be over in ten minutes to help. And will you make more coffee? I know you've probably finished one pot already, but I could *really* use some. And you should feel damn special that I'm even up this early to help you. Bye."

Maddie could only stare at the receiver in her hand after the resounding click. What was that all about? Then it hit her. Oh, no. Had she really agreed to go to that resort? For a full six days?

"Oh god, oh god, oh god," she gasped, as her mind began to whirl. "What did I do?"

She looked in the living room and saw the shopping bags lying right where she'd dumped them yesterday. The too frilly, too see-through, too revealing clothes Kris had talked her into.

It hadn't been an ice cream-induced nightmare.

Maddie was still expecting to wake up by the time her plane took off. Only after she landed did she realize exactly what Kris had gotten her into.

Chapter Two

ഇ

Her first clue should have been the resort's shuttle-bus driver. A gorgeous specimen of male perfection, he'd been wearing a tight white T-shirt and equally snug blue jeans. At the time she'd thought the attire was a bit unusual for a uniform, but as a female, she'd certainly appreciated it. It had also brought to mind Kris' comment about the possibility of hot, single males.

By the time they arrived at the spa, Maddie was feeling a little better about the whole thing. It was only for a week. She could relax, be pampered and let someone else cook for her. Since she was already here, she might as well make the best of it. Her finances would survive, despite her indulgence.

Looking up at the driver, she couldn't help but once again admire his physique. She dared to wonder if he'd explore the pleasure garden with her. If he looked that good in his jeans, she knew he'd look even better out of them. Who knew, maybe with the help of a few martinis she might even work up the courage to ask him.

The shuttle pulled to a stop as she continued her musings.

Any ability to think rationally left her when the driver hopped out and suddenly shucked his clothes.

Maddie's jaw dropped along with the driver's well-worn denim. Wow. She had no idea how he fit *that* in a pair of jeans.

It was one thing to fantasize, but this was a little bizarre. Disconcerted, and impressed despite it, she watched him nonchalantly adjust the straps on his skimpy leopard-print thong. Tight buns flexed as he trotted around back and hefted her luggage out. Unable to do anything but stare, she watched him carry the impressive package. And her luggage.

Wow again.

He looked up and caught her staring. Even then she couldn't seem to draw her gaze away from his...his...wow. With a wink and a dimpled smile, he said, "I'll take these straight to your room for you. And if there's anything else you need from me, just ask for Matt."

Blushing furiously at being caught staring and still confused, she could only think, *what in the world*? Before her brain had a chance to comprehend, she was approached by a perky brunette. A nametag attached to a barely there bikini top proclaimed her to be Shannon. She was perky just about everywhere, Maddie couldn't help but notice.

"Welcome to Hedonist's Paradise, Ms. Summers. I hope your flight went well." Shannon didn't wait for a response. "We have you staying in one of the Desire bungalows. It's one of our best."

"Hedonist's Paradise?" Maddie asked, momentarily finding her voice.

"Home of the world-renowned erotic spa and resort," Shannon replied proudly.

"Erotic resort?" she parroted again, and glanced around wildly. Was anyone else listening to this?

Perky Shannon nodded enthusiastically. "Yes. I can guarantee your stay here will be unforgettable. It's our promise to you. Why don't I show you to your room?"

Maddie followed in a daze. An erotic spa and resort. Was this supposed to be some sort of sick joke? For Kris' sake, it had better be.

She stared straight ahead in an effort to ignore the partially and fully nude men and women meandering, dangling, bobbing and jiggling about.

As Maddie stumbled along beside her, Shannon steered them along a wide path that took them past various bungalows. "You can see that our bungalows are arranged in little circles. Each group surrounds its own garden and has its own theme."

Since Maddie was still stuck on the "erotic resort" part of the explanation, she could only nod in response.

Pointing to the nearest one, Shannon went on. "That's the Tropics. The garden has white sand, palm trees and various tropical flowers, complete with a small turquoise pool. Over there is the Lodge. You can see the bungalows look more like log cabins, complete with cozy fireplaces. The garden features more evergreens than flowers and has a manmade stream that winds around it. It's pretty popular with the men who want to experience some of the outdoors while still being able to get a massage and play a round of golf. It's their idea of roughing it."

Maddie couldn't stop a strangled laugh from escaping. She'd just spotted a couple locked in a passionate embrace and the woman was busy stroking the man's dick. Which, incidentally, was out in the open for anyone to see. She waited for someone to comment, but no one seemed concerned with the flagrant display.

Baffled, shocked and disturbingly curious, Maddie watched the woman stroke the impressive erection. Was that thing even real? And did that come with the room? Stifling another hysterical laugh, she looked back at Shannon.

Shannon nodded, misunderstanding Maddie's humor. "I know it seems silly. But they're mostly city dwellers who want to experience a bit of nature. Some of the men find the outdoor setting to be a turn-on."

Certain she was trapped in an alternate dimension, she followed Shannon in stunned disbelief.

Continuing with her small tour, Shannon said, "We arrange the bungalows in small groups for the guests who have similar…desires. That way they're able to be together in a more intimate setting than a hotel, yet still have the privacy of their own room. As well as the numerous amenities we offer."

Maddie didn't even want to think about what those might be.

"Ah, here we are."

They stopped in front of a bungalow that was more the size of a small cabin. Shannon opened the door and waved Maddie inside.

"I'm sure you'll be pleased with this one." She gestured toward the sliding glass doors. "Out back you'll find a pleasure garden with over three dozen different varieties of fragrant flowers planted throughout that help to create an aromatic as well as romantic setting. There's also a large hot tub designed to look like a natural hot springs, and a gazebo with a swing. You'll probably have it mostly to yourself because three of the Desire bungalows are under renovation right now. So that leaves you and the guest in the next room to enjoy it. Do you have any questions about your room?" When Maddie didn't respond, Shannon headed for the door. "Well, if you don't need anything else right now, I'll leave you to settle in."

"Wait a minute!" The words came out in a desperate voice. Struggling to control her rising hysteria, Maddie tried to speak calmly. "Actually, um, I think there's been some sort of mistake." Which was a huge understatement. "My friend set this up for me and—"

Shannon smiled widely. "Of course. Kris called earlier. You don't have to worry about a thing. We'll take good care of you while you're here."

Relief coursed through her. Kris must have called ahead and set that whole scene up as a joke. And she'd fallen for it. Though the horny couple had been a little much, even for Kris. Then again, maybe she'd imagined it all. Shaking her head ruefully, she thanked Shannon.

"My pleasure." Shannon turned back at the door. "One more thing. On the nightstand you'll find a list of the spa treatments that come with the resort package. At your convenience, just call the number listed to set up the appointments. We also have twenty-four-hour room service. Or you can take your meals at one of our two restaurants, both of which I highly recommend. Otherwise, if you need anything else, you can call the front desk and ask for me. Enjoy your stay." With a little wave, she was off.

Once she was alone, Maddie took a minute to survey her room. The main focus was the four-poster, king-size bed, which dominated one side of the bungalow. She peeked into the bathroom, which boasted a jetted tub that could easily hold three people and an equally generous shower with two showerheads. To balance the ambiance were a wet bar, fireplace and posh furniture. This was definitely more sophisticated than she was used to.

The décor was soft and stylish with various pale greens and soft lilacs, lending a romantic quality to the room. Which was exactly what they were going for, Maddie thought wryly.

"I may not experience any romance while I'm here, but I'm definitely not going to let this place go to waste," Maddie said aloud. Giving the room another once-over, she laughed. "Erotic spa and resort. That's a good one."

Picking up the paper Shannon had pointed out, she looked at the list of spa treatments. She couldn't remember the last time she'd had a pedicure or massage. Scanning the list, she felt her jaw drop once more. This couldn't be right. Her anger mounting, she flipped the paper over, hoping it was another joke.

Toe Fetish Pedicures.

Full Body Massage with Oral Stimulation.

Manacled Manicure.

Chocolate or Whipped Cream Body Wrap with Special Tongue Bath.

Eyes bugging, she grabbed the small book that described the resort's fitness activities. It was even worse.

Beginners Kama Sutra. Advanced Kama Sutra. Naked Yoga for Couples. Nine or Eighteen Holes of Swingers Golf. Nude Nature Hikes.

The list went on.

Falling from nerveless fingers, the book hit the floor with a dull thud. Maddie didn't know whether to laugh, yell or cry.

Damn Kris. What in the hell had she been thinking, sending her to this...this... Her angry thoughts stumbled to a screeching halt. Wait a minute. Kris had known exactly what she'd been doing. She was always after Maddie to stop working so hard and go out. Find a guy. Have sex. And then rinse and repeat.

Kris was every inch the hedonist. She lived life with no other goal than to enjoy it, something she frequently urged Maddie to do. The impromptu vacation should have sent a huge red flag up in her mind.

Angry and humiliated Kris would even think to send her to a place like this, she picked up the phone. Stomach churning, she was determined that Kris would get her out of here.

Now.

As she suspected, all she got was an answering machine. Slamming the phone back in its cradle with a scowl, she furiously wondered what to do. There was no point in shouting at an answering machine. And even shouting at Kris wouldn't change the fact that she was stuck at an erotic resort.

"Okay. Enough of this," she admonished herself aloud. Freaking out wasn't going to help when what she really wanted to do was rail at Kris. She'd paid an arm and a leg for this vacation. So far she'd gotten a leopard-print thong and a real live porn performance in return.

With a long sigh of defeat, she slumped onto the bed. There was no way she could give this vacation up. Partly because the resort had a no-refund policy and partly because it still hurt to think that her best friend thought she'd been "living in a shell".

Besides, she tried to reason, *what was the worst that could happen*? In her mind's eye, she recalled the overly amorous couple. Okay, could it really get worse than that? It wasn't like she had to participate in the nude hikes or *Kama Sutra* lessons. All of the activities were optional. She could simple do her spa treatments and sit in her room and drink martinis for the duration of her stay. Alone. Though maybe not naked.

Determined to make the best of the unbelievable situation, she once more picked up the spa treatment list. The print seemed to grow larger on the page the more she stared. Was this stuff even legal? Skimming the options, she saw smaller print at the bottom of the page. *Traditional spa treatments also available.*

Hmm…

Maddie walked to the sliding glass doors that led to the pleasure garden. It really was beautiful here. If one could ignore the occasional glimpse of naked men and women engaged in various sexual acts. She let her head rest against the glass.

This was ridiculous.

She was here to relax and enjoy herself. If that enjoyment included naked people then she'd just have to deal with it.

No wonder Kris had threatened to sneak into her luggage. The Whipped Cream Body Wrap with Tongue Bath would probably have been right up her alley. The thought brought a small smile to her face. Maybe this vacation wouldn't be too bad after all.

She heaved a sigh of resignation. There was nothing to do now. Kris would most likely be conveniently unavailable for the next few days. No, she'd simply have to make the best of it, which meant it was time to get settled in — though she refrained from unpacking most of her clothes in case she needed to make a quick getaway.

Glancing outside, she noticed the sun was about to set. A twinge in her lower back reminded her of the long flight. Now was as good a time as any to try out that hot tub. Her clothes could be dealt with later.

A quick search in her luggage led her to the bikini. She couldn't help the look of disgust that crossed her face. This purchase had definitely been a weak moment for her. A weak, pathetic moment — when she had allowed Kris to get the better of her yet again.

A bikini woman she was not. She had never felt comfortable showing that much skin at one time. But there was no help for it now. She put it on and threw a short silk robe over it. But not before she'd self-consciously peeked in the mirror.

The verdant print definitely brought out the green flecks in her eyes. It was the halter top that Maddie had an issue with, which increased her already generous cleavage. Not to mention the Brazilian-cut bottom that showed just a little too much of her backside. Then again, Shannon had said she had the place to herself, so why did it matter?

After a slight hesitation, she took off the robe and grabbed a towel instead. She could handle an almost-nude body during an evening dip in the hot tub. Heck, she was going to be in a pleasure garden at an erotic resort. A skimpy bikini should be appropriate, if not too much clothing. Shannon had said there was only one other guest next to her. More than likely it was another woman here to enjoy the spa, so she really had nothing to worry about.

Stepping through the slider, she was soon immersed in fragrant blooms of various sizes. There was just enough light left for her to be able to appreciate the delicate beauty of colors surrounding her. She stopped to touch a petal here, sniff a fragile blossom there.

"Amazing," she murmured softly. And it was. She could barely see her room now, as the garden had been designed to provide privacy from passersby.

Maddie knew the difference between a tulip and a rose, but the variety of flowers in this place astounded her. Their scents blended to create a heady, almost sensual aroma. It was the perfect romantic setting.

With a wistful sigh, she moved farther along the narrow path, which had opened up into a small clearing. Shannon had said a hot tub, but the manmade rock pool sitting before her wasn't what she considered a hot tub. It was larger than a swimming pool, with small alcoves perfect for a couple to steal away in. Steam lazily wafted off the smooth surface as she moved closer.

Maddie threw her towel over a rock and eagerly stepped in. A moan of pure pleasure was drawn from her as she slid into the warm water. In unconsciously sensual movements she made her way deeper into the pool.

Some wonderful person had seen fit to create a small ledge around the edge of the pool so she could sit back and close her eyes. She lifted her arms to rest them on the rocks. This had to be the closest to heaven she'd ever been.

* * * * *

Ash couldn't move.

He hadn't been able to move since she'd first slid into the water. Except for his dick, which had gone from zero to hard in two seconds flat. Hell, he couldn't blame his body's reaction. She was a beautiful water nymph come to life. He couldn't remember the last time he'd reacted to a woman this way, if ever.

His erection pulsing in his hand, he watched with fascination as she expelled a soft moan and leaned back into the water. When she'd put her arms on the rocks, it had lifted her generous breasts partially out of the water. The tips of her nipples peeked through the surface every now and then as the water lapped at her. Envious of the water, he continued to look his fill while he stroked himself.

Her hair was pulled back, but he could see it was a rich brown, with hints of red. Would it reach her shoulders when down, or would it tease her nipples? The small of her back maybe? He was determined to find out.

Her skin looked so soft and creamy. A perfect dessert for his starving taste buds. The image of her long, long legs and gently swelling hips would be permanently etched in his brain. Her skimpy excuse for a bikini had shown him she was padded in all the right places. Exactly how he liked them. He only hoped this one was available for the taking.

What he wouldn't give to take her right now.

First he'd slowly slide the straps of her top down and feast on those perfect tits while they bobbed in the water. With the liquid heat swirling around them, he'd… *Easy boy*, he warned himself. A few strokes from completion, he removed his hand regretfully. If he was going to come, he'd much rather be inside her luscious heat than inside the hot tub.

He'd only been here one day and already this place was getting to him. This was supposed to be a working vacation. He was actually here to see if the resort was worth investing in and take a few days to relax on top of it.

The whole idea of an erotic resort had made him laugh. How many people really came to a place like this? According to the figures they'd sent him, quite a few. So he'd come to look things over. But he'd gotten much more of an eyeful than expected.

When he'd first stepped into the lobby, he'd been welcomed by a topless woman with obvious…enhancements. After dumping his bags in his room, he'd been given a whirlwind tour of the grounds. Along the way, he'd seen a couple having sex on a bench, a number of people engaged in what had looked to be a group grope-and-suck session, a nude step-aerobics class, and a roomful of more leather and chains than he'd ever wanted to see. He'd been propositioned more times than he could count and for various sexual acts. None of which had interested him, though some had been amusing.

Ash was interested now, and not in the least bit amused. He didn't care why this woman was here, but if she wanted to have an erotic experience, he was more than willing to offer his services.

Figuring it was time to stop being a voyeur and announce his presence, he moved forward and cleared his throat. "Ahem."

The nymph jumped and looked around wildly. "Oh! You scared me. I didn't know there was anyone else here."

"Sorry," he murmured.

At the moment he wasn't inclined to say more. He'd been half afraid she'd disappear into thin air if he moved. Blinking his eyes just to make sure, he began breathing again when she remained in his vision.

As he moved closer, he could see her studying him.

Good.

He hoped she liked what she saw. When he was only a few feet away, he said, "I'm Ash."

"Hello there, Ash. I'm Maddie. I guess you're the other guest staying in the Desire bungalows." Was that a hint of trepidation he heard in her voice?

The smile he flashed her could only be described as predatory as he replied, "I guess so. Are you here alone, Maddie?" Almost cringing at how blunt that had been, he wondered where his manners had gone. Then he remembered where he was. Manners be damned.

He held his breath while waiting for her answer.

She said nothing for a moment, and he wondered if she would answer or start screaming for help. Finally, her sweet lips uttered the one word, the only word he wanted to hear. "Yes."

Chapter Three

ɛɔ

Maddie couldn't believe she was sitting in paradise talking with the most gorgeous man she'd ever seen. The faint light peeking through the foliage hinted at gray eyes fringed by long lashes. And this was one instance where she knew they hadn't been wasted on a male.

Thick dark hair was slicked back from his face. Because it was wet, she wasn't sure if it was black or a dark brown. Either way it was gorgeous.

He was gorgeous.

The planes of his face were chiseled, almost to the point of being severe. Almost. It was his lips that helped to soften the image. Thin and masculine, with the lower lip slightly fuller, she's seen the killer smile they curved into. She had a strong hunch that those lips could probably do quite a bit more than make her knees weak with a simple smile. Oh, the possibilities they inspired.

Maddie was a little shocked at the territory her mind was veering into. Daydreaming was one thing, but he was her fantasy come to life.

Though his body was mostly hidden underwater, she guessed that his broad shoulders tapered to a lean waist. And a whole lot more.

And his voice. Oh my. It was oh-so sexy and rough and deep. Her name had never sounded so good coming from anyone else. He had a perfect bedroom voice. The kind of voice a woman wanted to hear last thing at night and first thing in the morning. In fact, Maddie could only imagine the amazing things he could whisper in her ear. Sweet nothings, sexy, dirty phrases and anything in between.

The hungry look in his eyes made her shiver. No man had ever looked at her that way, especially not one who could model for *GQ*. He was staring at her as if…as if he wanted her.

Badly.

But no, that couldn't be right, could it? Dismissing the thought as wishful thinking, she decided it must be the reflection off the water.

Either that or he hadn't eaten dinner yet.

The silence had continued long enough to become awkward. Maddie searched her mind for something, anything to say.

"So, ah, what brings you to the resort?" As soon as the words left her lips, she wanted to snatch them back. Of all the dumb, unoriginal things to say. Why else would a guy come to a resort like this?

"I needed to get away and relax."

Relax how? she wanted to ask. Instead, she decided on a safer topic. "Me too. I haven't had any R&R in a long time. I have a feeling after a few of the spa treatments I'll be feeling much better." Too late, she remembered what sort of "treatments" they offered. Blushing hotly, she shut her mouth.

The gleam in his eyes became speculative as he gave her a quick once-over. "Yes. I can imagine."

In a rush, she tried to explain. "No, no. I don't…I mean, I'm not… Actually, my friend sent me here as a joke. I thought I was coming to a regular spa to be pampered and instead she sent me…here," Maddie finished lamely.

"Ah. So you're not here to…partake in the activities?" The question was laced with curiosity as well as interest.

She shook her head firmly. "Not the activities you're thinking of." Though after seeing her neighbor for the week, she couldn't help but rethink her decision.

"Pity." With one simple word he managed to arouse her and challenge her. The warm water couldn't disguise the heated longing that rushed through her.

Pity? What did that mean? Was it a pity she wasn't interested in having some stranger suck on her toes, then buff them, or was it a pity she wasn't here to have sex?

Tipping her head to the side, she studied him. If there was a way to make this week of indulgence any better, here he was. Kris had said she needed to live a little. A vacation fling was as close to living on the edge as she could get. Since she was stuck here for the duration, she'd certainly need something to do. As they said, when in Rome…

Maybe she should sleep with this one.

On this one. Maybe she should sleep *on this one*, she mentally corrected. After her body had cooled down enough to let her brain resume working, she might be able to come up with an idea to make this work.

The silence stretched on and Maddie quickly lost what little nerve she had.

Deciding retreat would be the best course of action for the time being, she found her voice and forced cheerfulness into it. "Well Ash, it was nice to meet you, but I'd better head back. I had a long flight." With as much dignity as the scanty bikini would allow, she stepped out of the water. Why oh why hadn't she brought the stupid robe?

"Maddie?" he queried softly.

She wrapped the towel around herself before turning around. "Yes?"

"I promise I won't bite. Unless you ask me to."

Wow. The images that immediately came to mind were X-rated and much more tempting than she cared to admit…

Steam swirled around them as their naked bodies pressed together. Maddie loved the feel of his chest hair against her sensitive nipples. Bending her back over his arm, he nibbled his way down her neck. The only sound to break the silence was her soft moans of encouragement.

The heat of the water was ignored as a need much hotter consumed them. His dark head was beneath her chin as he took delicate love bites along her collarbone. When he reached her breasts, she held her breath. His teeth came closer and closer to her nipple as her longing grew. Her hands tangled in his hair, insistently urging him closer.

The first bite took her by surprise. He'd pulled her nipple deep into his mouth. Without warning, his teeth had closed down around the delicate peak. She cried out at the delicious pleasure he invoked.

Her head dropped back as he tugged gently. A shiver snaked up her spine when he used his tongue to soothe the sting. Moving to the other breast, his teeth grazed the underside of the creamy skin…

The image was so vivid Maddie felt her nipples tighten in response. Her mouth opened and closed a few times but no sound came out. Without another word, she whirled around and practically ran for her room, dignity be damned. The sound of his low laughter filled the night, following her.

* * * * *

In the safety of her room, Maddie quickly changed into her pajamas and robe. An outfit that offered much more protection than the bikini had. So why was it she felt more exposed than she could ever remember feeling?

The mirror reflected the image of her flushed face. Unfortunately, she knew she couldn't blame it on the mad scramble to reach her room, coward that she was. No, it had everything to do with the sexy man in the hot tub and the temptation he presented.

And was she ever tempted.

Very, very tempted.

His sexy eyes had promised things she knew he'd be more than able to fulfill. Dropping into a cushy chair, she considered her possibilities. This week was supposed to be all about her. And while she was enjoying the benefits of the spa, why couldn't she also enjoy a vacation fling with a gorgeous man? This was supposed to be about giving the old, conservative Maddie a rest and letting the new, liberated Maddie have fun. She'd been conservative in areas of her life other than her clothing and spending habits.

God only knew how long it had been since she'd had sex. Two years, seven months and three days. But she wasn't counting.

Granted, her dry spell was by choice, or more honestly, because she hadn't had the time, but it wasn't as if she hadn't been interested. There just hadn't been anyone suitable to satisfy her needs. Certainly the only two men she'd ever been with hadn't been able to satisfy them.

Her only sexual experiences had been big disappointments, compliments of James and Trent. Two men—more like boys— she'd met in college. She'd still been a virgin when she met James. All her friends had had sex, so she figured she'd see what the fuss was about. During the momentous occasion, she'd only been able to think about the project she needed to complete for her history class. Afterward, she'd wondered how soon she could get him to leave without sounding rude.

Obviously not a great moment.

When she'd met Trent, she was sure that he would at least keep her attention. Which he had. Although it hadn't been his witty charm or talented hands that had done it. No, it was because he had squealed like a stuck pig throughout the deed. Moans and groans or even shouting she could have handled, but squealing?

Needless to say, Maddie had been a little gun-shy ever since. She wanted to find a man who put her pleasure before his. Which, for her, had been a lot easier said than done.

Until now.

Maddie had a feeling that Ash was a man who could show her pleasure. Real pleasure. And he'd already started with the delicious heat in the pit of her stomach that increased in intensity when she remembered the look in his eyes, the timbre of his voice. Just thinking about him gave her more pleasure than she'd ever received from a man. And he didn't seem like a squealer, so that also gave him an edge.

After everything that had happened, it was galling to admit Kris just might be right. Though she hated to admit she'd been living in a shell, she did realize her social life was nonexistent. At this point, she did deserve to have some fun. In fact, it was long overdue. If nothing else, she was honest with herself. The conservative role she'd placed herself in hadn't been making her happy. Maybe this place would help her true nature to emerge. Whatever that might be.

With a smile, she made her decision. Tomorrow she'd find Ash and give him a proposition he'd be sure to accept. Remembering how she'd run from his flirting, she *hoped* he'd accept. If he did, this vacation was sure to be the best she would ever have. Besides, it would only be for a few short days and then she'd be back to her normal routine. It would be safe and satisfying. No attachments, no complications, just hot, steamy sex.

In the privacy of her own room, of course. She was ready to test the waters with Ash, but she wasn't ready to experiment in front of a group of horny strangers.

Swapping the chair for the bed, she nearly moaned at the heavenly softness of it. In minutes, she was asleep. Blissfully unaware that the object of her dreams was currently having a much more difficult time.

* * * * *

Ash groaned in real pain as he hopelessly tangled the sheets on his bed trying to get comfortable. He'd figured a nice cold shower would help dampen the effect she'd had on him.

What a damn sorry time to be wrong.

His erection hadn't been this encouraged since...since never. Not when his hormones had raged out of control as a teenager. Not even when he'd been a favorite among the sorority girls in college. And especially not in recent memory, when he'd treated sex more as a basic function, like eating or sleeping. Unfortunately, he'd gotten more enjoyment out of his last meal than his last bed partner.

Yes, he'd finally gotten to the age where meaningless sex held no appeal for him. At thirty-two he didn't consider himself old, but he did realize that life moved a hell of a lot faster than a guy expected it to. With everything going on, suffice to say it was time to start thinking about his future.

He was tired of coming home to empty rooms. Tired of working himself to death because he had nothing better to do. And he was tired of the string of women in his life who only wanted sex, his money or both.

Ash wanted more. What he wanted was a life. A future. A woman he could pleasure and take pleasure from, in every sense of the word. The chestnut-haired beauty made him realize there was hope for him yet.

Though he'd only been in her company for a few moments, it was all he'd needed. Maddie intrigued him in a way nothing and no one ever had. Granted, his first reaction had been gut-wrenching lust, but he'd also been captivated by the hint of innocence in her eyes, the inherent grace of her movements. Not to mention the flash of awareness and desire he'd seen in her gaze. All of which had awakened the primitive urges in him. Hell, he was surprised he hadn't beaten his chest and dragged her off by her hair. He shook his head at the ridiculous image.

Yes, the sexy, tempting Maddie called to him on many levels. Some of which he hadn't realized existed until now. But he was so very glad they did. Because he'd already decided what to do about it.

He'd always been decisive. That's exactly what had gotten him where he was today. In the business world, he was reputed to have an uncanny sixth sense which allowed him to size up a situation in a relatively short period of time and decide a profitable outcome. His accuracy was nothing short of miraculous. And right now his sixth sense was telling him that Maddie was, without a doubt, someone he needed to get to know better.

His throbbing erection agreed wholeheartedly.

Groaning again, he rolled over and punched his pillow. In the meantime, he'd better try to get a little rest. He had a seduction to plan. And the odds were against him considering she'd run from him tonight. Ash was nothing if not tenacious when it came to getting what he wanted. And he always got what he wanted. Right now that was Maddie, and everything she stood for in his life. Keeping that in mind, he clenched his teeth, ignored his body's raging desire and settled in for a long, sleepless night.

Chapter Four

෨

She could see the gleam of his eyes in the moonlight. They were hungry. He was hungry. And she was the main course. Never had she felt so hunted, or so wanted. The combination brought on a heady, sensual feeling.

A delicious shiver worked its way up her spine.

"Come here."

The soft command was delivered in a voice so deep, so compelling, she couldn't help but obey. Maddie wanted to obey. She had an overwhelming desire to know exactly what his tempting-as-sin voice offered her. Part of her knew. Another part of her wondered how far he'd go and how high he'd take her. Further than she'd ever been, of that she was certain.

The water lapped gently in her wake as she glided slowly to where he sat, never looking away from his intent gaze. Her heartbeat accelerated the closer she came. She stopped when she felt his thighs surround her waist. His erection brushed against her stomach. The temptation to slide onto him weighed heavy in her mind. The fit would be perfect. The feel of him would satisfy a deep-seated craving she'd only recently discovered. But she'd let him set the pace.

Kneeling before him in the hot tub, she waited.

Warm hands came up to stroke her arms, her shoulders. His touch set her nerves on fire. She craved the sensation as it heated a response within. Down her back, his hands continued to stroke, deftly untying her bikini top along the way. The straps slid off her skin as he let the top drop into the water.

Her nipples puckered as the cool night air caressed her skin. The contrast was a shock to her system. But it was his touch that made her catch her breath. His hands cupped her breasts, testing their fullness as they filled his palms. Rough thumb pads brushed her nipples, drawing a low moan from her lips.

Eyes half closed, she almost missed the satisfied smile he flashed at her cry. Not to be outdone, she brought her hands to his chest. She was done waiting. Repeating his gesture, she lightly flicked his nipples. He bit off an oath and drew her closer.

"Maddie," he groaned, his deep voice heavy with need. She could feel his erection, hot against her stomach, pressing insistently. Reaching down, she gently took him into her hands.

An involuntary shudder was his only response as she began to stroke him below the water's surface. She wanted more. Slipping lower, the warmth of the water moved over her head as she sank under water. Eyes closed, she moved her mouth lightly along his shaft. She lifted her head to draw a breath and he gave her no time to think as he pulled her onto his thigh. She could feel the hairs on his leg against her mound as she straddled him, her hands returning to caress his penis.

His hips moved in time with her strokes as her hands deftly squeezed and stroked, bringing him closer to the edge. His thigh moved up as well, pushing firmly against her heat. The resulting friction was perfect and she unconsciously began to undulate against him. The corded muscles of his thigh rubbed against her clit. She moved her hips faster, needing the delicious release.

In a quick motion, he pulled away from her hand and positioned her above him. She threw her head back as he entered her in one quick thrust. He filled her completely. His eyes glittered as he lifted her up and down. She saw her own out of control hunger mirrored there.

Cupping her breasts in her hands, she watched him closely. Her hair was dripping wet, and a few droplets fell onto her collarbone. They trickled down her left breast. Raw need sharpened the planes of his face as he watched their descent. Smiling at his enraptured expression, she offered him a nipple to feast on. Drawing her deep into his mouth, he suckled hard, causing her inner muscles to clench him tight.

They groaned simultaneously at the sensation. He lifted his head and growled, "Give me your mouth."

Their mouths met in a scorching kiss. Maddie pressed herself closer. Just as she was about to wrap her arms around his neck, he pulled away slightly.

Ash pulled out and turned her away from him. Wearing a slight frown of confusion, Maddie allowed him to guide her to the edge of the hot tub. He placed her hands on the edge of the hot tub and slid his own down to her hips. His knee pressed between her legs, forcing them gently apart. When she was spread just enough, he slid his dick inside her.

She lay back against his chest as one of his hands came up to cup her breast. He placed his other arm around her waist and began to move inside her. Because she couldn't see him, she let her eyes drift shut and focused instead on the feeling.

Lifting her left arm, she brought it around to hold his neck, her right hand moving down to her clitoris. Ash was nibbling lightly on her neck as she began to caress herself. With only a small touch, Maddie could feel an orgasm building.

His hips moved faster and he held her tighter as he neared his own release.

Maddie felt him drop his head to the crook of her neck as he grasped both of her hips and drove his dick harder and deeper inside her.

Her orgasm was an explosion of sensations as she cried out into the still night around them. Her heart beat furiously against her chest as she gulped in a deep breath. *Wow.*

He drew out of her slowly and turned her so that they faced one another. He opened his mouth to speak and…

Maddie woke with a jolt to the horrible sound of the bleating alarm clock. She looked around, slightly disoriented. "What in the world?" She slapped at the stupid clock ineffectively.

Was it just her imagination or was the noise getting louder? With a muffled curse, she groped for the plug and pulled it from the socket.

"Oh…my…god," she mumbled into her pillow. Part of her wanted to yell in frustration. Another part of her was a bit worried that she was already having sexy dreams about the Adonis from last night.

Stumbling toward the dresser, she rummaged around until she located her watch. It was only 6:30 in the morning. With a sigh, she shook her head. It was probably a good thing the alarm had been on, otherwise she would have slept through breakfast. And Maddie on an empty stomach was not a pretty sight.

Pushing the erotic dream from her mind and desperately ignoring the lingering desire humming through her body, she looked around for salvation.

She found it in the form of a small coffeemaker. She picked up the packets of coffee to see what her choices were. Ragin' Javaholic, Coconut Delite, and Breakfast Blend in regular or decaf. Tossing the others aside, she started the Javaholic. Though it wasn't a brand she recognized, with any luck it would live up to its name.

Ten minutes later, she was feeling a little better after a hot shower complete with massaging showerhead. Images of how that showerhead would come in handy with her vacation hunk had her distracted while she took a quick sip of coffee. Or tried to. The images of a wet, dripping Ash were immediately replaced with shock. Choking and wheezing, she tried to breathe past the tar filling her throat.

"Oh, gross," she gasped.

With a baleful stare at the coffee mug, she read the empty coffee packet. "Ragin' Javaholic. You've hit the caffeine mother lode."

She grimaced at the cheesy slogan and muttered, "More like, you'll have the mother lode of all caffeine hangovers if you choke this nasty stuff down." That one sip was going to be enough to see her through to next week.

Shuddering, she dumped the remaining coffee in the sink. If she felt like touching coffee again this week, she'd definitely stick with normal blends.

Selecting a new yoga tank and matching pants, she hastily put them on. After securing her hair in a loose ponytail at the nape of her neck and dabbing on a small amount of lip gloss, she went in search of breakfast.

Anything to get the taste of caffeinated asphalt out of her mouth.

Maddie followed the scent of food and quickly found the large dining room where breakfast was being served. The assortment of breakfast foods was impressive to say the least.

Arranged artfully on platters were various pastries, from blueberry muffins to mini croissants covered in a delicate glaze. Next to those sat bowls of fresh fruit so perfect it looked unreal. A guest could choose from hot pans of hash browns, bacon, sausage or even a made-to-order omelet.

Pots of assorted coffee sat waiting to fill the mugs, but she was still a little gun-shy after the Javaholic.

Maddie filled her plate with slices of melon along with two of the mini croissants. There were only a few guests in the dining area and she spotted a table for two in an empty corner. Not wanting to chance sitting by any amorous couples, she weaved her way through the tables and sat down with her back to the entrance.

Unsure what to eat first, she stared at her plate. Upon closer inspection, she realized the fruit was sliced in the shapes of various body parts. For some reason, she didn't quite have the courage to slide the cantaloupe penis into her mouth this early in the morning. The mini croissants looked harmless enough, so she grabbed one and took a bite. Finding it delicious, she quickly ate the second on her plate.

She was debating the honeydew breasts when a voice interrupted her. "Is this seat taken?"

Her mouth formed an O of surprise.

She wasn't quite ready to see her gorgeous neighbor. She hadn't figured out how she would approach the subject of a fling, let alone if she would even go through with it. Looking down at her plate, she grimaced. Discussing anything over a plate of X-rated fruit just didn't seem right. Especially when said fruit made her remember the feel of him, hot and hard in her hand. Or how perfectly sculpted his thigh had been against her.

Regardless, here he was. Looking much too sexy in his formfitting T-shirt and khaki shorts. Oh Lord, the shirt outlined a set of pecs that had her nearly drooling. His shorts stopped right above knees that were preceded by a set of rock-hard calves dusted with dark hair. His waist was narrow in comparison to the broad shoulders, just as she'd imagined. He was still perfect even in the early morning sun. Oh yes, this man would be something to explore for hours, even days.

By the time her perusal made it to his face, his lips were quirked in an all-too-knowing smile and his eyes danced with humor along with something else. Another thing she wasn't quite ready to get into at 7:15 in the morning. Not over a plate of penises.

Realizing she hadn't answered him, she took a fortifying breath. "Um, no. It's all yours."

Still stunned by his appearance, she could only watch as he sat and began eating his omelet.

Settling back in her chair, she watched him eat. She'd read love scenes where a woman would seductively eat grapes, or strawberries dipped in whipped cream, or even popsicles. But who knew a man eating his breakfast could be arousing? She certainly hadn't. The corded muscles in his throat worked with each swallow he took. His lips closed around his fork with such relish she could only feel envy for the metal prongs. His tongue swept out over firm lips... She looked down at her plate before he could catch her staring again.

Big mistake.

On her plate was a depiction of a man and a woman, limbs entwined. The paper squares her pastries had sat on each described a different *Kama Sutra* pose. In great detail.

Eyes wide, she stared at the pictures long enough for her vision to become blurry. A deep chuckle brought her back to the present.

"Interesting reading material you've got there. I usually go for a newspaper myself, but I think you might be on to something." He picked up one of the small papers. "Hmm..." Twisting it one way, and then the other, he stared at it thoughtfully. "I'm not sure if that even looks comfortable, let alone enjoyable. What do you think?"

She took the paper he offered gingerly. "Um...well, I don't really know..." she let her words trail off. Her body was practically humming with arousal. Either that or the caffeine jolt had done more damage than she first thought.

His lips quirked. "You never know unless you try. But it's still early and I'm not that flexible to begin with. How about we explore one of the walking trails instead?"

Explore? Oh yeah.

She wanted to explore every inch of him. Take her time and really... It took effort on her part, but she brought her focus back to the present conversation. "This morning? Ah...okay, sure."

"Great." He drank his cup of juice, once again bringing her attention back to his throat. If she ever got the chance, she was going to find out if his skin tasted as good as it looked.

He stood and held out his hand. "Shall we?"

She took one look at the cantaloupe penis, which was listing slightly to the left. Placing her hand in his, she looked up with a soft smile. "Lead the way."

* * * * *

As soon as she put her hand in his, Ash knew he was a goner. Her face was freshly scrubbed and free of the heavy cosmetics women seemed to rely on these days. Except for the peach-colored shine she'd put on her lips. He could have tasted that for breakfast and satisfied his hunger.

Well, maybe only sated his hunger, because he wouldn't have stopped at that. He would have had to sample the creamy skin at her collarbone. And the sweet little belly button he remembered so vividly from last night. It was difficult to veer away from that particular train of thought.

Ah, it was good to feel again.

Not only lust, but a sincere interest. He wanted to know all of her secrets. Her likes and dislikes. He wanted to know about her family, her career. What made her happy or sad? What areas of her body did she like kissed, licked and caressed? He wanted to know every little detail about what made her tick.

Ash led her out of the resort and onto a path similar to the one that led to their rooms. "One of the staff recommended this path for a morning hike. He said it was spectacular."

He watched her look around at the beautifully landscaped grounds and smile. "I'd have to agree with him so far. This place is unbelievable."

As he stared at her dazzling smile, he could only agree with her assessment. "Absolutely incredible."

A rosy hue colored her cheeks when she caught his meaning, which surprised him. He hadn't known there were women left in the world who still blushed with modesty. The women he attracted were mostly gold-diggers who relied on their physical assets, natural or cosmetically enhanced. Mostly the latter. The only blush to color their skin was the kind you had to apply with a brush. The sort of women who became upset if a man didn't immediately pay tribute to her beauty. Maddie obviously didn't fall into that category. A fact that couldn't have pleased him more.

Rather than draw attention to her embarrassment, he merely tightened his hold on her hand. They continued on in companionable silence, content to admire their surroundings and enjoy the peaceful morning.

The silence was broken by a loud moan. They stopped in their tracks when they saw where the noise was coming from.

The couple who'd helped to greet Maddie yesterday was locked in yet another torrid embrace. Only this time, the woman's shirt was on the ground.

Too shocked to move, Maddie stared, mouth agape. As the couple parted from their kiss, the man dipped his head to taste the bared breasts in front of him. The very large breasts. Letting out a low moan of pleasure, the woman tipped her head back. She was obviously savoring the touch. Maddie felt her own nipples tighten in pleasure. It was impossible not to picture herself and Ash in their place. His dark head bowed in front of her, his hands on her flesh.

Dropping to his knees, the man pushed up the woman's short skirt and spread her legs. His tongue slid between her folds, causing her to cry out in pleasure. Her hips bucked wildly as his mouth continued to feast.

Maddie squeezed her legs together in a hopeless attempt to stop the moist heat dampening her panties. In her mind's eye, it was Ash's tongue on her clit, inside her, making her cry out in helpless pleasure. Unconsciously she swayed closer to him, her breast brushing against his arm. Heat radiated off his skin as he stared beside her. Oblivious to their audience, the couple continued their lovemaking. When the man stood and swiftly thrust inside his partner, Maddie turned her head, not wanting to spy further. Desperately fighting her desire to copy their actions.

Ash gripped her hand tightly and tugged. Nodding his head in the opposite direction, he led her away quietly. Body still thrumming, she followed. Not for the first time wondering exactly where he'd lead her.

He spied a small bench, one that put them out of sight and earshot of the couple. Steering her toward it, they both sat down heavily.

Had they stayed one more minute, he would have had her pressed up against the nearest tree, making her moan loud enough to wake any resort guest still asleep. Hell, he could already taste her on his tongue. He could feel her heat squeezing his erection. He could… Jaws clenched, he took a few deep breaths. It was neither the time nor the place, despite what his body wanted.

Damn, did he ever want her. He'd spent all night knowing she was only a room away. He'd tried to read the file he had on the resort, but seeing the activities they offered hadn't helped. The numbers had looked great, but his mind hadn't been able to focus on anything but Maddie.

Neither spoke as the minutes passed. Finally, needing to break the tense silence, Ash tried for normal conversation. He had to clear his throat a few times before he could ask, "So, are you a morning person?"

Maddie was evidently ready for a change of subject as well. She chuckled at his question, though it was a tad strained. "Only after I've had a pot of coffee." She closed her eyes and inhaled deeply, savoring the fresh air, still struggling for control. "Actually," she continued, "I'm one of those early-to-bed, early-to-rise sort of people. I'll admit I'm not at my best, but I get better with each sip of coffee."

"Ah, so you're a caffeine junkie?"

"No, not really. It just makes it a little easier to get going in the mornings." Ash grinned at the admission. She caught his eye and smiled ruefully. "Okay, I guess I'm a bit of a junkie. But I only drink it in the mornings at home. That has to count for something, right?"

He pretended to consider her words. "Well, I suppose then we can't technically label you a junkie. I think that's more along the lines of merely being caffeine dependent."

Maddie laughed at his teasing, relieved she was regaining her ability to think clearly. "Gee, thanks. I'm glad we cleared that up."

They sat in silence once again. Listening to the sounds of the morning around them, minus any moaning. He could occasionally hear people walking along the path, taking advantage of the beautiful weather and great hiking. And who knew what else. He wondered if the exhibitionist couple was still at it. Then again, maybe it was best to forget about that whole scenario.

Eventually Ash turned to her, curious to know more. "Maddie, tell me about yourself."

"What do you want to know?"

"Anything. Everything."

He could tell his answer made her self-conscious, but she gamely replied, "Okay. I'm twenty-seven. I'm a Taurus. I love ice cream and hate green beans. And at my last checkup, the vet said my teeth looked good."

For a moment he could only stare at her. Then a wide grin split across his face. Beautiful Maddie had a sense of humor *and* a sassy personality.

Oh yeah, this was definitely the woman for him. Modest, with a touch of spunk. It was an arousing combination. Trying to ignore the confining material of his shorts, he managed to reply in turn, "I'm thirty-two and a Scorpio. I hate tofu and love seafood. And at my last checkup the vet proclaimed me healthy as a horse with the stamina of a stallion."

She blinked at him, and he figured she was at a loss for words. Hell, he was at a loss for words.

Had he really just said something so idiotic?

The stamina of a stallion. What was more pathetic than that? He'd been out of the dating scene for a couple of months, but that was just pitiful. Never had he wanted to recall his words quite as much as he did right now. Where was his cool head and suave charm when he needed it? He could blame it on the fact that all of the blood that normally supplied his brain was currently in his dick.

She surprised him when she merely said, "You love seafood and you have the stamina of a stallion. Does your diet consist of a lot of oysters?"

Now it was his turn to blink at her. When she erupted into laughter, he couldn't help but smile, though it was with chagrin.

At least he'd managed to break the ice. And though he was tempted to explore the topic of aphrodisiacs in great detail, he was more interested in learning about her. "Yeah, well. Let's try this again. What do you do for a living?"

Wiping a tear from her eye, she was still chuckling when she said, "Right now I'm an office manager at an architecture firm."

"Really?" His brows rose.

"That surprises you?"

"I don't know. I guess it does."

"What, you were able to figure me out after our brief meeting last night?" she teased. At his shrug, she admitted, "Well, it's definitely not what I want to be doing for the next twenty years. Or even the next five. But the pay is pretty good and I have great benefits. For right now it suits my purposes."

"That makes sense," he nodded. "What happens when you've finished there? What's your dream job?"

The wistful expression in her eyes gave him pause. "My dream job? Most people would probably say they want to be an actor, or doctor, or even a stockbroker. Something exciting and glorified that makes a person more cash than they can spend in one lifetime."

"But not you?"

She gave a small shake of her head. "Nope. I've never wanted to be rich or famous. Too much pressure. Actually, I've been saving money so I can open my own bookstore." She pressed her lips together suddenly, as if she'd said more than she'd intended.

He was intrigued. "What sort of bookstore?"

After a slight hesitation, she replied, "I've always wanted to own one of those cozy little bookstores with the overstuffed chairs where a person can sit and read for a few hours at a time. And of course I'd have a small eating area where you could order lattes and treats, like cookies or muffins. I'd keep all of the current bestsellers on stock, with a selection of secondhand books as well." One shoulder came up in a slightly defensive gesture. "I know it isn't the most lucrative choice of businesses, but it's something I've always wanted to do."

There was no way he could have missed the excited gleam in her eyes as she had described her vision. Though she had obviously expected him to scoff, he merely smiled. "I think it's a great idea. Too many people go for the money instead of following their dreams and they end up unhappy."

"You sound like you speak from experience." Her gaze was questioning.

He grimaced. "You could say that. Either way, I wish you luck." Hoping to move away from the subject, he stood abruptly and asked, "Should we walk a little more?"

"Sure."

Taking her hand, he walked back to the path and began to stroll at a leisurely pace. He mulled over what she'd said moments before. If only she knew how important her words had been to him. And how she was going to help him fulfill a few of his own dreams.

His thoughts were interrupted when she turned to him and asked suddenly, "Would you like to have dinner with me tonight?"

Ash wanted a hell of a lot more than dinner from her tonight. However, he remembered the trace of wariness he'd seen in her eyes last night. As he wondered how to temper his response, he watched her smile fade with disappointment. Damn, not what he'd wanted.

A slightly wicked smile curved his lips. "Are you providing dessert?"

Her shy, but steady gaze met his in spite of the loaded question. "Definitely."

Ash smiled with satisfaction at her soft reply. It had been quiet, but sure. It was exactly what he'd needed to hear. "I'd love to."

Chapter Five

&

Ash had walked her back to her room shortly after agreeing to dinner. The feral smile he'd given her had made her shiver. In anticipation.

She was still amazed she'd been able to ask in the first place. Even more amazing was how she had blurted out her dream about the bookstore. It was a secret she usually kept to herself.

It was a little disconcerting to realize she was interested in more than just his body. Their walk this morning had been unexpected. When she'd made the decision to seduce him, talking hadn't been part of the plan. But he was so easy to talk with. After the initial awkwardness had passed, that is. They had continued discussing trivial things on the walk back to the bungalows. He really seemed to listen to what she had to say. Her intuition told her his interest was genuine and not simply a pretense to get her into bed.

Before she could let herself start to think about what a great guy he could turn out to be, she had to strengthen her resolve. Regardless of his conversation skills, getting to know him wasn't a good idea.

It would make this vacation fling a lot harder to deal with when she left if she started to like him as a person. Instead of only wanting him as a man. If she began to develop…gulp…feelings for him, things could get a little messy. At least with her emotions. How awful would it be to find the perfect guy and only have him for a week? The last thing she needed was to be nursing a broken heart.

This wasn't the sort of place a man went to start a relationship. People were here for pleasure. Thinking back on the scene they'd witnessed on their walk, she thought some guests were having a much better time at it than others.

No, in order to make this work she needed to stay away from anything personal and concentrate on everything physical. She had to. She'd simply forget about the way his sexy gray eyes had stared intently at her while she'd described her bookstore. Or how he'd asked questions as if he really wanted to get to know her. Or even the way her hand had felt nestled in his while they'd walked.

With a sigh of disgust, she shook her head. At least she could try to distract herself with thoughts of something, anything else. According to her watch it was 9:30 a.m. Tonight was a long way off. Grimacing, she wondered what she could do to spend the time.

The spa would be open by now. Some serious pampering sounded like the perfect distraction. A quick phone call later, she had an appointment for a haircut and facial. Both, she'd been assured, were the traditional treatments and were done completely clothed.

When she walked through the glass doors half an hour later, an attractive blonde with perfectly tweezed brows and a nametag that said "Bree" looked up from a large, curved desk with a rich mahogany finish. The lobby was small, with overstuffed loveseats and a variety of magazines atop a glass coffee table. It was cozy and much tamer than Maddie had anticipated. Which made her a little wary as she stood at the front desk. A perfect smile graced the receptionist's perfect face and she said in a perfectly cultured voice, "Hello. How can I help you today?"

Determined not to feel inadequate next to the beautiful Bree, she merely said, "I'm Maddie Summers. I have a ten o'clock appointment for a facial and hair treatment."

"Oh, Ms. Summers, Jacques is all ready for you. Would you like anything to drink? Water, tea?"

"No thanks. I'm fine," Maddie replied, wondering if she dare order a shot of whiskey. Her nerves were still a little on edge from Ash. The fact that everyone at this place was gorgeous didn't help either.

"If you change your mind, let me know. Jacques is back this way if you'll just follow me." She led Maddie to a small room past the front desk, where a slender man with a shock of bright red hair was waiting. A vase overflowing with peonies sat atop a glass counter and a salon chair was placed directly in front of a large, gilt-framed mirror. Maddie took a moment to admire the peonies, then looked back to see Bree exiting the room with a small wave. Her eyes unwilling strayed to Jacques.

She'd seen red hair before, even considered her own hair to be red in certain lighting, but this was *red*. Perhaps a shade darker than Ronald McDonald red. Oddly enough, he pulled it off. Maybe it was the leather pants or the seven silver studs in his ear that made it appropriate. Or maybe he simply had the right attitude to carry it off. Either way, she didn't know any woman that could pull off a color like that and still look good.

She was still waiting for her eyes to adjust to the sight of him when he rushed over to her with a megawatt smile. "Ms. Summers! I'm Jacques and I'll be working with you today. Are you feeling adventurous? Because I'm thinking a few inches off the ends, some color and lots of layers! Oh, I can see it now. You'll look fabulous when I'm done!"

Color? Layers? No, she was more than happy with her little trim every eight weeks. Her stylist had tried a few times to talk her into subtle highlights, but Maddie had been adamant. Hairstyle trends seemed to change as frequently as clothing fashions. Which was much too often, in her opinion.

A person could go broke simply trying to keep up with them. Her hair may not be the latest look, but it worked for her. And it was easy and inexpensive to maintain, another bonus. Plus, there was no way she was going to let anyone with hair *that* color change hers. She'd probably end up with green hair or white highlights. Suppressing a shudder, she opened her mouth to tell him what she did and didn't want done with her hair and to order a stiff drink. But before she had a chance to respond, she was whisked into the chair and tipped back for a shampoo.

When Jacques put his fingers in her hair, words were quickly forgotten. The man had magic fingers. Absolute magic.

If this was the traditional treatment, she knew she wouldn't survive the erotic one.

He gently massaged her scalp with a luscious, coconut-scented shampoo. Her eyes closed in bliss as his fingers continued to relax her. If scientists ever perfected cloning, this was one guy they could make dozens of. Maddie decided if his talents with styling hair were anything like this, he could do anything he pleased to her.

Maddie relaxed in the chair, giving herself over to his care.

Three and a half hours later she was gazing at the mirror in awe.

Jacques hadn't been kidding when he said her hair would look fabulous. He'd trimmed her bangs so they lay in delicate wisps around her face while the rest fell in a cascade of layers across the tops of her shoulders. The golden highlights he'd added gave her hair and skin tone a warmer appearance, while the hair treatment had made her tresses shiny and soft.

Maddie turned her head and watched her hair sway in an attractive arc around her face. Her skin was freshly exfoliated, cleansed, moisturized and had a light layer of artfully applied makeup. The facial had been over an hour of paradise. After Jacques had finished the color, she'd been placed in the hands of a highly skilled esthetician and her skin had never looked or felt so good. All too soon it had been over and she'd been placed back in Jacques' talented hands for her hairstyling. No one had let her look in a mirror until it was all done. And she hadn't been disappointed. Between her hair and her glowing skin, she felt like a new person. By the time she actually went home, she *was* going to be a new woman. And so far she loved the transformation.

She quickly went to schedule the rest of her spa treatments.

Back at the front desk, Bree looked up with a smile. "All done? Wow, you look great! Jacques is a wonder with hair, isn't he?"

"The man should have his hands insured. He's amazing," Maddie agreed with a heartfelt nod. Now she would be able to tell Kris that one man had managed to satisfy her using only his hands. Wouldn't she be jealous?

Jacques had come up behind her. "Sweetie, you have gorgeous hair and bone structure that was just dying to be shown off. All I had to do was make a few snips and voila!"

"I still have a manicure, pedicure, body wrap and massage to schedule. You don't by any chance do any of those, do you?" she asked hopefully.

He laughed and shook his head. "Sorry. My talents are limited to hair. But I recommend Mandy and Jared for those. They're just fabulous! You'll love them!"

Although she was disappointed, she took his advice. Again, after assuring that they were the traditional treatments. Bree made the appointments and handed her a reminder card. "Here you go. We'll see you back on Wednesday for the body treatments and Friday for the rest."

Maddie took the card and left the spa, loving the feel of her hair softly swinging against her neck. It was now quarter to one and her stomach was reminding her she hadn't yet had lunch. As happy as she was, she could probably even stomach a phallic-shaped entrée. Who knew, maybe it would prove inspiring.

She decided to try out the resort's more casual restaurant. A relaxed atmosphere was achieved with soft instrumental music and soft, cushy seating. Maddie found the normalcy a tad strange, considering the servers were dressed in nothing more than a small apron. It certainly made for an interesting contrast.

The menu boasted cuisine full of fresh fruits and vegetables. She settled for a cold gazpacho soup with a side of fresh fruit and an iced tea.

While waiting for her food, she took the time to study the other guests in the restaurant. She was surprised to find a fairly diverse crowd. There were a few couples who appeared to be at retirement age, a group of middle-aged women, a few business men with Palm Pilots in hand as well as a handful of younger singles. This place definitely attracted all types of people. Maddie wasn't sure if that was a good thing or not in this case.

The waiter came back with a frosty tropical drink of some sort and set it down in front of her.

"Oh, this isn't mine. I ordered an iced tea."

"Compliments from the gentleman," he replied, and handed her a small note.

Compliments from the gentleman? Maddie opened the note and scanned the contents. It simply read, "For a beautiful lady."

So Ash was sexy *and* sweet. A potent, not to mention dangerous, combination. But she couldn't suppress the slight blush that stained her cheeks. Scanning the room once more, she was disappointed when she couldn't see him.

As she craned her neck trying to locate him, she was surprised to turn around and see an attractive man with blond hair standing at her table.

With a polite smile in his direction, she continued her visual search.

He cleared his throat. "I hope you like the drink."

Confused, she looked at the drink. Realization suddenly dawned and this time her cheeks were blushing from embarrassment. How foolish she was to automatically assume the drink had been from Ash.

Her smile slightly warmer, she replied, "Oh, thanks. It was thoughtful of you." Maddie hoped that sounded gracious enough without appearing interested.

57

Unfortunately, he seemed to take it as an invitation and slid into the opposite chair. Flashing a set of pearly whites that had obviously seen a bleach treatment or two, he offered his hand. "Cole Hawthorn."

"Maddie," she offered somewhat reluctantly, shaking the proffered hand.

"Well, Maddie, I couldn't help but notice such a beautiful woman dining alone. Dare I hope that you're here by yourself?" She was pretty sure the wink he gave her was supposed to be flirtatious. Unfortunately for him, it came across as a little too corny and somewhat sleazy. He was gazing at her expectantly and she realized he was waiting for an answer.

What in the heck was she supposed to say? She'd never been a big fan of lying, but in this instance, the truth probably wouldn't help her. Who knew what kind of weirdo sex fiend he might be? So she hedged. "I'm eating lunch alone today."

"In that case, do you mind if I join you?" Not bothering to wait for a reply, he signaled to the waiter.

As he placed his order, she tried to make sense of what was happening. An attractive man had bought her a drink and had invited himself to eat with her. And all she wanted to do was eat and run.

What was wrong with her?

Any other normal red-blooded woman would be flattered instead of faintly nauseous. He really was good-looking in a pretty boy sort of way. But her taste had never run toward pretty boys. No, her taste ran more toward sexy, dark-haired men who gave new meaning to the word testosterone.

Blond pretty boys must give her indigestion. That would explain the nausea. The only other plausible explanation was that she was already much too attracted to a certain dark-haired man. A man she'd just met. Nope, it had to be indigestion.

If she had been worried how she would get through the meal, his running monologue neatly solved the problem. She learned more about Cole Hawthorn in ten minutes than any one person would ever want to know. Information that ranged from what country club he was a member of to what sports he'd played in high school. She chose to ignore the not-so-subtle comments about his preferences and prowess in the bedroom. Her hearing had effectually shut down after he had started his lengthy monologue on whips, chains and gags. Ugh.

When the waiter finally brought their food, she could have kissed him. A mouthful of food should keep her annoying lunch companion quiet long enough for her to scarf down her food and make her excuses.

No such luck.

In morbid fascination, she watched him fork a pile of linguine into his mouth. Sauce dripped down his chin which, now that she noticed, was somewhat weak. Linguine noodles hung out of the corner of his mouth until he noisily slurped them up. Ugh again.

He finally noticed her scrutiny and smiled. Only it suddenly looked more like a leer. Maybe it was the piece of green...something in his white teeth. The great bleach treatment now only served to emphasize the spot of green. Either way, she found her appetite had deserted her.

It was probably just as well, because he had once again started to talk about himself. Around the un-chewed food in his mouth.

Maddie tuned out what he was saying and instead tried not to focus on the food stuck in his teeth, which she could swear was growing larger by the mouthful. No matter how hard she tried, she was unable to look away.

Mistaking her disgust for interest, Cole's leafy smile turned shrewd. "Maddie, I was wondering if you'd like to join me later. My room is equipped with some items you might find...enjoyable."

A masculine hand appeared on the table beside her and she ignored it, trying to hold back the bile that had risen in her throat.

"Sorry I couldn't make it for lunch, dear. My golf game was running a little behind schedule."

Thankful she recognized that voice, Maddie was extremely happy to look up and see Ash. "Oh, that's—that's okay."

Cole blinked at the two of them in confusion. "I thought you said you were alone."

"No, I said I was eating lunch alone today," Maddie said, fighting to keep the grateful smile off her face. She hoped Ash would play along with her next words. "My boyfriend loves to golf and he was so eager to play the course here, I was positive I wouldn't see him until dinner. Isn't that right, honey?" She blinked innocent eyes at him.

But he turned the tables with his reply. "As much as I love golf, you know I love you even more, pumpkin."

Now she blinked in wariness. Okay, that was laying it on a little thick. And had he really just called her pumpkin?

Cole was looking at her again with suspicion. She'd never aspired to be an actress for a good reason. She couldn't act to save her life. However, dire circumstances such as these called for desperate measures. Pasting on her most winning smile, Maddie gave it a go. "Cole here was nice enough to buy me a drink and keep me company while I ate. Wasn't that sweet of him?"

"It sure was. But if you don't mind…Cole, was it? I'm going to steal her back now. It's been over four hours since I last saw her and we have some catching up to do, if you know what I mean." Ash punctuated the innuendo with a man-to-man look, and before she could utter another word he'd swept her out of the restaurant.

They were halfway to the bungalows before she had time to respond. It took a minute for her to regain her breath between giggles, and when she did, she could only sputter, "Catching up to do?"

His smile was not unrepentant in the least.

Maddie could only shake her head. "And did you call me pumpkin?"

Eyes twinkling, he continued to smile. "Isn't that what a boyfriend's supposed to do? Call you sickening little pet names. Come home from a round of golf and expect sex and a well-cooked meal."

That comment was a little more than Maddie could handle. Cheeks flushed with embarrassment—or maybe sexual tension—she turned and began to head back toward her room.

Ash caught up with her a few steps later. "Hey, I was just kidding. Aren't you going to thank me for saving you back there?"

She stopped and took a couple of deep breaths. Retreating back into her shell was the last thing she needed to do. Though she might seriously *want* to, she knew she shouldn't. Maddie expelled a long breath and gave in. "Yes. Thanks for rescuing me."

"Anytime. As long as I'm not playing golf, you can count on me, pumpkin," he couldn't resist adding.

She surprised him by laughing softly. "Yeah, yeah. I'll get you your meal tonight...sweetie pie."

"Touché," he said with a smile.

She looked up at him and their eyes met. The smiles slowly faded from their mouths as the lighthearted mood faded. He'd asked her earlier if she was providing dessert. Maddie wondered if they could skip right to it now.

Gray eyes were watching her carefully. Desire flared between them and the conversation was quickly forgotten. Maddie couldn't help but wonder why he affected her like he did. Why now, why here?

He reached up and slowly twined a strand of her hair around his finger. "I like your hair," he said quietly.

"Thanks. It's a new style for me." She was nervous now, and had to stop herself from babbling more of the obvious.

His only reply was a quirk of his lips.

The fluttering in her stomach increased with that slight movement. Sensuality seemed to vibrate off him in tangible waves. As he continued to gently feel her hair, she desperately tried to regain some semblance of control over her scattered thoughts. "I really do appreciate you intervening when you did." It was the only thing she could think to say.

"Glad I could help. I'm just relieved to know that you really did want rescuing."

She stared at him questioningly.

"I suppose most women would have found him attractive and I didn't know if you might be one of them. Besides, the name of the game here is pleasure," Ash explained. He seemed a little embarrassed to have even brought it up.

Maddie shook her head. "No, I have no interest in men whose conversation skills are limited to 'me, myself and I'. Not to mention the fact that his table manners are more appropriate for a barn." For a moment, she thought she might have seen a flash of relief in his eyes. But it was gone so quickly, she couldn't be sure. Unable to stop herself, she had to add, "Besides, my tastes these days are running more toward tall, dark and handsome."

His eyes widened a fraction and he sucked in a deep breath. Then a slow smile formed as he gave her a look that promised retribution of the sweetest kind. Maddie could feel an answering response in the pit of her stomach where a desperate longing was building. Instinctively their bodies swayed near, their mouths drew closer. Her brain had all but stopped when eagerness for his kiss had taken over. She closed her eyes and waited a tense moment for their lips to touch.

When nothing happened, she popped one eye open and saw him looking away from her. She followed his gaze and saw a group of women laughing their way down the path to where she and Ash stood. None of them were wearing tops. They both looked away, uncomfortable with the sight. Or maybe it was the emotions running between them, Maddie couldn't be sure.

By the time the women had passed, the mood was definitely broken. Maddie took little pleasure in the fact that the muscles in his jaw and neck were corded tight with frustration. Heck, the muscles in her whole body were tight with frustration.

He took her hand and led her back to her room. "As much as I hated the interruption, I certainly don't want our first kiss to be in public. Not here, anyway."

"Oh," was all she could manage. So he did plan on kissing her, just not in public. She was fine with that. Despite the fact that anything seemed to go here, she wasn't into public displays either. She wanted him all to herself. And if all went well, kissing would only be the start of it.

Maddie hadn't realized she was smiling until he gave her a strange look. "What's that smile for?"

Her first instinct was to clam up. But the new Maddie was much more daring and after a heartbeat, she finally replied, "I was thinking that it's a good thing we were interrupted."

"And why's that?" he all but growled.

She waited until Ash looked directly at her, then smiled. "Because I wouldn't have wanted to stop at just one kiss."

It was gratifying to hear the breath hiss sharply between his teeth. His grip on her hand tightened as well. Thankfully she wasn't the only one affected by this tension.

When they reached her room, Ash grabbed her key card impatiently and ushered her inside. She turned around expecting him to be right behind her, but was surprised to see him standing outside the door. "You're not coming in?"

He smiled ruefully and shook his head. "I can't. I have a massage scheduled in about twenty minutes and if I come in now..." he trailed off, but Maddie knew what he was leaving unsaid. "Besides, we have a dinner date tonight, don't we?"

"Oh, yeah. We do." How in the world could that have slipped her mind? She still had to figure out what to wear, shave her legs, and do all of those other things a woman had to do before a big date. It would also give her time to take a step back and gain her bearings. She was in way over her head with this one.

"Did you have anything specific planned?" When she shook her head, he continued casually, "I was thinking maybe we could order room service and have a more private setting."

Room service? Private setting? It would certainly make this seduction a whole lot easier for her. She was unaware of the small smile that touched her lips as her mind filled with possibilities. "That sounds great. What time works for you?"

The siren's smile she was wearing nearly shattered his control.

This woman was slowly killing him. Ash wanted nothing more than to let her finish the job. Though his body thought right now would be best, his ever logical mind saved the day. "How…how about six?" he had to stop and clear his throat over the desire threatening to choke him.

"Perfect. I'll see you then." Before she shut the door she thought to say, "Enjoy your massage!"

He watched as the door shut slowly in front of him. After a minute, he forced his feet to moved, walking slowly toward the spa.

That smile.

God that smile.

Women shouldn't be allowed to have smiles like that. Smiles that make a man forget who he is, where he is. Didn't they know that men were defenseless when it came to their desire for women? Well, in his case it was one woman in particular, but still. She might as well be a harem full of women with the power she held over him. Which was dangerous for him this early on. Even though he meant to have her permanently, he'd have to be careful.

Very, very careful.

If she found out just how much he was affected… Ash groaned at the thought. Regardless, tonight she'd discover the depth of his feelings, both physical and emotional. It would either send her running in the opposite direction or she'd use it to her advantage.

He was preoccupied with those disturbing thoughts when he reached the spa. The woman behind the counter gave him a friendly, if somewhat appraising smile. "Hello. May I help you?"

"Ash Delaney. I have a massage scheduled." His clipped tone discouraged any propositions.

Her eyes lowered in disappointment and she skimmed through her appointment book. "Mr. Delaney, it'll be just a moment. Courtney is finishing up with her previous client. You can have a seat over there if you like." She pointed to a group of overstuffed leather chairs. "Would you like something to drink? We have coffee, tea, water, soda…?"

"No thanks." The only thing he wanted right now was back at the bungalow. And he'd have to wait until tonight to sample her. Shifting in the chair, he tried to find a more comfortable position for his rampant erection. A constant state for him since he'd met Maddie.

He was given about ten minutes to gain a degree of control before being led back to a massage room. Once alone, he quickly stripped down to his briefs and lay on the table. Normally he would have stripped completely. But because he seemed to have no restraint over his own body it was best to keep things under wraps.

Literally.

Hell of a lot of good it did him twenty minutes later when he found himself thinking of the hands massaging him as Maddie's hands. He hastily tried to rein his wayward thoughts in, but it was too late. Still on his stomach, he could feel the telltale growth in a certain part of his anatomy that was quickly becoming a huge source of frustration. *Okay, okay*, he silently amended, *it was a big frustration already.*

He knew that erections were a common sight at this place, but damn, he should have a little more control at his age. He wasn't here to sample the various…morsels, he was here on business. At least he had been until he'd met Maddie.

The massage therapist was busy with his feet, so he only had a moment or two before she'd ask him to roll over onto his back. His briefs were black cotton that barely concealed the necessaries. What to do? Work always had a decent cold water effect, so he mentally began reviewing files he'd been working on before he'd left.

When that didn't work, he cursed his underwear. They provided support when a guy was relaxed, but what about when he wasn't?

Ash was pretty sure he wasn't the only guy out there to ever wish he had a little more support at times like these. He really thought he'd gotten past this stage in his life. Then again, had he ever been this horny? Not until Maddie.

Dragging his mind back to the present dilemma, he wondered at the unjust differences between men and women. A woman would never have this problem. Sure, women's nipples hardened when they were aroused, but that could also be excused to cold temperatures. And he definitely couldn't say a cold breeze had caused this. Aside from draining his body of testosterone, there was nothing that could have prevented this. Or was there?

He'd once dated a woman who modeled underwear and hosiery. Looking back, he was pretty sure she'd talked about a new line of control-top pantyhose and briefs she'd had to model. They'd had some sort of control panel, whatever that was, to help keep everything in. It had worked as a constraint of sorts.

Hmmm.

Wouldn't something like that work for men?

Ash thought of the possibilities. Just think—a pair of briefs that worked to keep everything in the right place at all times. Or at least all the times a guy needed it to. They would have a panel to help keep things from bulging...

With a frown, he backtracked.

A guy wanted a bulge of some sort, just not an inappropriate one. So it would have a strategically placed panel to help keep a man's natural shape, while restraining a potentially embarrassing situation. Yeah, that was good.

But what to call them?

It would have to be something catchy...like Bulge Binder Boxers. No, that could be mistaken to mean it would minimize a man's assets. What man wanted that? Ash thought for a moment and smiled. What about Erect Correct Briefs? That was good. But it would need a slogan too. Something like "We'll keep you in place while you keep your pride". Or maybe "You control the conversation and we'll control the rest". Or how about "Holding you back until you get the green light"?

Ash was so intent on his idea he was surprised to hear the massage therapist say, "Mr. Delaney, you might want to take a moment before you stand up. As soon as you're ready, I'll have a bottle of water for you out front."

He was done? He didn't even remember rolling over onto his back. And he was happy to find the situation was back to normal.

All thanks to Erect Correct Briefs.

Laughing, he shook his head. If he ever needed to change careers, maybe he should look at going into apparel. At least now he had something to occupy his mind the next time a problem arouse—ahem...arises. But at the rate he was going, he'd have mentally completed a full business plan by Thursday.

Shaking his head once again, he dressed quickly and left the spa. He was eager to get back to his room and get ready for his dinner date. Ash only hoped he'd be able to get through dinner without creating an expense report and buying inventory for his new idea.

Chapter Six

ଅ

Maddie checked the clock for the fifth time. 5:40. Only two minutes later than the last time she'd looked, with twenty minutes left to kill. She could always look at the room service menu.

Again.

Actually, she was fairly sure she could rattle off the list of entrees with her eyes closed. Maybe she should order wine. But would he like red or white? Or what about champagne? No, that would be too much for a first date.

Oh, who was she kidding? The whole purpose was to wine and dine him. A nervous giggle escaped. Clapping a hand over her mouth, she stifled the sound as she thought about how ridiculous that sounded. Rolling her shoulders to help ease her anxiety, she decided to wait so they could order drinks with their food. No use working herself into a nervous wreck. Any more than she already was, that is.

A glance in the mirror showed a beautiful woman in a short, fitted dress. The simple sheath had thin straps that barely held up a low neckline, showing off the tops of her breasts. The hem stopped well above her knees and moved considerably higher when she sat, barely covering the tops of the sheer stockings held in place by a skimpy garter belt. The matching bra and panties were a delicate pink lacy material. Material that exposed much more than it covered. She loved how the racy garments were softened by the candy color. Hopefully Ash would have a sweet tooth. He had, after all, asked if she was providing dessert tonight.

Resisting the urge to look at the clock again, she moved around the room to make sure everything was picked up. Before she could begin her third round, there was a knock on the door. The clock read 5:45 as she went to open it.

Oh. My. God.

With her mouth slightly open, she stood there staring at the gorgeous hunk of masculinity gracing her doorway. Her heart skipped a few beats, then resumed at an accelerated pace as the rest of her body responded with wholehearted feminine approval.

Yum.

Ash was wearing a dark blue polo shirt and a dressy pair of khaki slacks. His black hair had enough waves to curl recklessly around his ears and at the nape of his neck, which had her fingers itching to run through it.

The man looked hot.

The name Ash fit him perfectly, because she was pretty sure if she touched him right now, she'd go up in flames. There was nothing cold or gray about him. Even his molten silver eyes seared her with their intensity.

"Hi," he said quietly, in that deep, sexy, guaranteed-to-make-you-shiver voice.

"Hi yourself," she replied, somewhat breathless. When he continued to stand there, she shook her head. "Oh, sorry. Come on in."

As he walked into the room, she was avidly aware of the way his clothes looked as if they'd been tailor-made for him. What she wouldn't give to be those slacks. Lovingly cupping his…

"Here, these are for you." He turned and handed her a bouquet of flowers. Not your typical roses, it consisted of a wild array of flowers and colors. Lovely, yet unusual.

She loved them.

"Thanks. These are beautiful!" She inhaled their fragrant aroma, trying to get a grip on her wayward hormones. They were already in a vase, so she placed them on the nightstand where she could see them from anywhere in the bungalow.

"You're beautiful," he said, drawing the words out as his eyes roamed her body in appreciation.

"Uh, thanks." Maddie could feel the heat in her cheeks from the compliment, one she wasn't used to receiving. As compliments went it was simple, but when Ash said it she really did feel beautiful. Especially when he said it with such heat in his eyes.

Unsure of what to do, she walked toward the small table, keeping her back to him. The momentary silence was deafening. What to do, what to do...

Her dating skills were severely limited, her seduction skills even more so. At the moment, she had no idea how to proceed. Her newfound courage had quickly deserted her. *Get a grip! You can do this.*

She took a few deep breaths to calm her racing pulse. It had been a while since she'd done so much heavy breathing. They hadn't even done anything yet! All it took was his presence and she was reduced to gulping air.

Finally managing to locate a thin shred of courage, she turned toward him. He was leaning against the door with his arms crossed over his chest. It caused her to momentarily lose her train of thought, as she stared at the sleek muscles rippling in his arms. Again, she could only think *yum*.

Ash was the one to finally break the silence. "So, what's on the menu tonight?"

"Whatever you want," was her breathless reply.

His hungry look nearly made her knees buckle. "Believe me sweetheart, we'll get to that later. But for right now let's concentrate on the meal."

Maddie was proud that her hand only trembled slightly as she grabbed the menu. Her knees were another story.

They made their selections and she called in the order. In five minutes she knew she'd never remember what it was she had selected. It would probably taste like cardboard anyway.

They had barely settled into a stilted conversation when the food arrived. They ate in uncomfortable silence, trying to temporarily ignore the desire sizzling between them. The food was delicious, but it was difficult to fully appreciate what she was eating. Not while Ash was sitting across from her. He seemed to be having the same problem and eventually they gave up.

Clearing his throat, he said, "It's nice out. How about a walk through the garden while there's still enough light?"

"Sure." A walk would greatly help to calm her nerves. She still wasn't quite sure how to proceed with the seduction. A walk in the pleasure garden would help to move things along, Maddie fervently hoped.

Hand in hand they strolled through the fragrant garden at an easy pace, their racing pulses a direct contrast to the peaceful, quiet night surrounding them.

It was probably against the rules of a vacation fling, but she wanted to know more about him. He'd asked her questions, so she figured it was only fair for her to do the same. Despite her earlier reservations and against her better judgment, she found herself saying, "Ash, you know a little about me, but I still don't really know anything about you."

"What do you want to know?"

"Oh, everything and anything," she repeated his earlier words to him in a joking tone.

"You already know I eat a lot of oysters," he teased.

She laughed, "Yeah, yeah. I can see I'll need to be a little more specific. Okay, what do you do for a living?"

"Ah. I'm a venture capitalist," was the curt reply.

"You don't sound all that thrilled about it." A fact Maddie found interesting.

He sighed and shook his head. "You could say that. It's a family company, so even at a young age it was expected that I would one day take the reins. And pretty much as soon as I graduated college, I did." He stopped to pick a flower. Sweeping her hair back, he gently placed it above her ear, along with a soft kiss on the neck. Nibbling slowly, he made his way down the soft skin of her neck. When he reached her collarbone, he lifted his head. Searching her eyes, he smiled, apparently satisfied with what he saw there.

While her pulse raced madly at the sweet, seductive gesture, he continued walking. "For the first few years, it was great. The company was already established, but I wanted to contribute my fair share. And I did. My family and business counterparts were all suitably impressed. The professional recognition was great for the old ego. And along with it came more money and women." The tone of his voice was now hard with cynicism. "There was an article written up in a popular local magazine about a year ago, and I was one of a handful mentioned in it. It was supposed to be about various business endeavors, but it became a list of eligible bachelors in the business world. Complete with estimated net worth."

"Judging by the tone of your voice, you must have been pretty popular after it came out."

His laugh held no humor. "You could say that. I had women calling me at home, and some even came to my office. I was asked out to dinner, the theater, you name it. And I went out with some of them. It was increasingly difficult to enjoy myself when I knew that they only saw dollar signs when they looked at me. None of them cared who I was or what I was like. It helped that I wasn't a decrepit old man, but even that wouldn't have deterred some of them."

The poor guy. She couldn't help but feel sorry for him. It was obviously a sore subject. Maddie tried to lighten his mood by joking, "Boy, how many men out there would love to have changed shoes with you for a day."

Instead, he remained pensive. "I know. There are a lot of guys out there who would love to have beautiful women waiting around every corner. And none of them would have cared that those same women were ruthless gold diggers who have no idea what love is. Women who would have jumped at a marriage proposal, but who also would have laughed at the thought of having kids. God forbid, a child would have ruined the bodies their plastic surgeons had worked so hard on. They were all so damned superficial and materialistic."

Maddie's heart ached at the anger and bewilderment in his voice. "Ash, I'm really sorry. I couldn't even imagine." She lifted a hand and held it to his cheek.

He stopped and looked at her with an enigmatic expression, placing his hand over hers. "No, you probably couldn't imagine. Which is exactly why I'm here tonight." Before she had a chance to think about his comment, he went on, "But I'm the one who's sorry. I'm sure that's more than you wanted to know."

"Hey, no problem. You were nice enough to listen to my crazy dream about my bookstore."

"I didn't think it was crazy at all. But I do appreciate you letting me unload my problems," he said with a rueful grin.

"Like I said, I don't mind." She steered the topic to another subject, hoping to erase the brooding lines at the corners of his mouth. "What about your family? Do you have any brothers or sisters?"

"No, I'm an only child. My mom was forty when she had me. I was what you could call an unexpected miracle. Both of my parents are still living. My mom had a bout with breast cancer a few years back, but thankfully it's in remission. And my dad is still hale and hearty and a tyrant in the business world."

Maddie could tell from the fondness in his tone that he and his parents were close. "I'm sorry to hear about your mom."

"Thanks. But here I go again, spoiling the evening with sad tales about my life." He looked around, taking note of the darkening sky. Night was closing around them and Ash turned them back toward the bungalows. "We'd better get in before it gets too dark to see. Then again, I wouldn't mind getting lost in the pleasure garden with you." Pulling her close, he swept his hands up her arms, down her back.

In a teasing caress, he cupped her buttocks, squeezing gently. He brought one of her hands to his mouth. Eyes intent upon her, he gauged her reaction as he placed a kiss on the back of her hand. It was a romantic gesture as old as time and Maddie was surprised at how arousing he made it. The soft brush of his lips teased her sensitized skin. Turning her hand over, he traced a fingertip along her palm.

Maddie held her breath as he took one of her fingers and placed it to his lips. He nibbled on the tip, watching as her lips parted. Drawing one into his mouth, he sucked gently. Maddie squeezed her thighs together against the answering pull in her loins.

Her breath hitched when he took another finger into his mouth. His cheeks hollowed as he sucked her fingers deep inside his mouth. The feel of his hot tongue against the pads of her fingers was highly erotic. Maddie had never known her fingers could be considered an erogenous zone. Then again, it could simply be Ash.

Very slowly, he drew her fingers out and placed a tender kiss to her wrist.

For a long moment, neither moved, absorbed in the passion growing between them. Ash tenderly brushed his thumb along her cheek and said quietly, "Let's head inside."

Back inside the bungalow, they found a bottle of wine and dessert waiting for them. "To top off the evening," Ash said. "I have to admit I have a bit of a sweet tooth."

Maddie gave an inward snort of laughter at his comment. How perfect, considering underneath her dress she wore garments designed to tempt him. But she merely said, "Hey, I never turn down dessert. I only wish they had ice cream flavors other than vanilla."

"You like ice cream? There's a little mom-and-pop ice cream shop near my office and they make the best ice cream you'll ever taste. I'll have to take you there sometime."

His words didn't really register because she was too busy imagining ice cream and Ash for dessert. She was having trouble deciding if he'd go better with double fudge or a chocolate-caramel swirl. Or maybe strawberry to match her bra. The intensity of his gaze eventually penetrated her musings and she looked up. The gleam in his eye was distinctly predatory. "Maddie, what exactly are your intentions toward me?"

"My...my intentions?" Her voice came out a squeak. That certainly wasn't a question she'd expected.

"Mmm-hmm." Ash began to walk slowly toward her. "I think it's a fair question."

She took an involuntary step back. "My intentions. Okay..." How was she supposed to answer that? And when had they gone from lighthearted flirting to serious stuff?

"Well, I don't intend to compromise your honor. And I can promise there won't be any reason for a shotgun wedding," she joked nervously. Searching his eyes, she found no trace of humor.

Okay, so the teasing approach hadn't worked. Lifting her shoulder in a deceptively nonchalant shrug, she took a deep breath and decided to give the truth her best shot. "Look, this vacation is all about turning over a new leaf, so to speak. I'm really attracted to you. Basically my intention is—was—to seduce you. I'm sure you could tell that I have no experience with this sort of thing. You're the first and probably the last since I don't usually do casual sex. But I have a feeling that if I left here without even trying to kiss you, I'd regret it for a long time. So there you go." Uneasy by the time she'd completed her little speech, she went and stood at the glass doors looking out at the garden. She seriously hoped she hadn't blown everything with her bumbling speech.

Positive he hadn't wanted to know quite that much information, she resisted the urge to lean her head against the glass. Maybe after he ran out the door she'd order another dessert from room service and raid the wet bar. Darn her stupid moral streak that thought he deserved the whole truth and nothing but the truth.

Without looking up, she knew he had come to stand next to her. "So you're looking for a vacation affair?"

Maddie was startled by the contemplative tone behind the question. "Um, yeah. I suppose you could call it that."

Ash stroked his chin thoughtfully. "I just want to be sure I understand exactly where you're coming from."

Ah, he wanted to make sure there were no strings attached. Maddie understood now. "All I want is a vacation fling. A few nights, that's all," she hastened to assure him.

He stared at her a full minute before answering. "No."

"No?" She couldn't have been more stunned. Had she read him wrong? She may not have had enough relationships to consider herself an expert, but she was pretty sure he'd been interested.

"No," he repeated. "You only want a few nights. I don't."

Comprehension dawned. "I see. Well, I'm sorry to have wasted your time." *And made a fool of myself,* she finished silently. "I'm sure you can find your way out."

Once again she turned her back to him, praying he would leave before the flush creeping along her cheeks betrayed her humiliation. So much for a steamy vacation fling. There was an obvious reason why she didn't date much, and he'd just witnessed it firsthand.

His hands came to rest on her tense shoulders and he gently turned her toward him. Valiantly trying to maintain her dignity, she faced him, determined not to be a coward.

The amusement on his face quickly fueled her embarrassment into anger. Before he could get a word in, she exploded. "You think this is funny? What in the hell kind of man are you? Do you get your jollies stringing women along? You think you're so sexy that any woman will just fall at your feet and offer herself to you, well let me tell you bud, I'm way too good for you." She resolutely ignored the voice in her head that oh-so kindly reminded her she had offered herself on a silver platter. Never mind the minor details. "Please leave. Now."

"Maddie, wait a second, let me explain." But she was already steering him out the door.

"Get out!" With a firm push, he was shoved out the door before it slammed in his face.

* * * * *

How in the hell had that happened? One minute she's telling him how she's going to seduce him, and the next he's staring at her closed door. Two inches from his face.

With a sigh, he raked his fingers through his hair. He'd royally screwed that up. She had mistaken his amusement completely. He didn't want only a few nights with her. He wanted *every* night with her. But she hadn't given him a chance to explain. Granted he had smiled at an inappropriate time since she'd just laid her pride on the line with her little speech, but it had been so refreshingly honest and sweetly naïve he hadn't been able to help himself.

God help him if he hadn't fallen a little in love with her because of it. What other woman out there would have so frankly stated her intentions? He'd had women say "I want you" or "let's go back to my place". But he'd never had a woman tell him she was trying to seduce him and that if she didn't try to kiss him she'd regret it for the rest of her life. Actually she hadn't quite said for the rest of her life, but it was close enough.

Yeah, he definitely had it bad for this contradictory, charming woman.

Realizing he was still staring at her door, he wondered what to do. Should he knock and try to explain? Should he give her a little time to cool off and then come back? Thoughts of the blond guy who'd been drooling over her in the restaurant made up his mind and he lifted his hand to knock. Before he could, the door swung open and Maddie ran right into his arms. Not one to question his luck, Ash wrapped his arms around her before she could escape.

* * * * *

After Maddie had kicked him out, the more she thought about the conversation, the angrier she'd become. Who did he think he was, laughing at her? She'd been honest with him and he'd all but thrown it back in her face. If he really wasn't interested, he could have just said so. In a nice way, of course.

Then she'd had the not-so-bright idea to storm over to his room and give him a piece of her mind. Instead she'd opened the door and run into him.

For a minute she could only stand in his embrace and breathe in the faint masculine scent of him. Why did he have to smell so good? And look so good? And be such a jerk? Steeling her resolve, she tried to pull away. While she'd been mooning over his scent, he'd wrapped his arms around her and he wasn't letting go.

"What do you think you're doing?" she demanded against his shirt.

"I'm going to hold you right here until you give me a chance to talk." As if to emphasize his statement, he briefly tightened his hold.

Two older ladies walked by on an evening stroll and tittered at the spectacle they were making. It probably looked as if they were locked in a passionate embrace. A foolish part of her wished they were, but her pride was still stinging.

Because he had such a tight hold, she couldn't quite look at his eyes, so she muttered into his shoulder, "Fine. But can we at least not do this out in the open? I've had enough embarrassment for one day."

Once they were in the room he shut the door. But he still wouldn't let go. She protested in a tight voice, "I really don't think this is necessary. I'll let you talk, then you can leave."

"Sorry, no can do. You're staying right here until I'm done."

But the jerk didn't sound at all sorry.

"You said you only want a few nights. Isn't that right?"

She laughed without humor. "No. I don't want anything from you or with you or whatever."

"Well, that's too bad. Because I want quite a bit from you and with you and a whole lot of whatever." He loosened his hold enough so he could tilt her chin up. "Maddie, I don't just want a week-long affair. It wouldn't be near enough to satisfy me."

Suspicion clouded her eyes, along with a huge dose of skepticism.

Hoping to convince her, he explained further, "You said you don't do casual sex. Well I have, and believe me you're not missing anything. It's empty and unsatisfying. That's not what I want with you."

He barely heard her soft "Oh". She pulled out of his arms and stared pensively at him. Then she frowned. "Ash, I don't know if I can give you more than that. And how can you even know if you'll want more with me when we haven't even kissed yet? Maybe the chemistry between us won't be there tomorrow."

Not even dignifying that with an answer, he gently grasped her chin and kissed her. As his lips skimmed across hers, he tried to memorize the shape of her lips. Not wanting to forget a single detail.

The soft brush of his lips sent a tingle through her. A sensual haze fogged her mind as she lost herself in his arms. Sighing lightly, she moved closer. A moment later she heard his muffled oath and suddenly found herself crushed against him.

The tone of the kiss went from inquisitive to wild, insistent. His tongue demanded entry and when she granted it, he showed her how erotic a kiss could be. With sensual skill, he gently sucked on her bottom lip before tracing the contours of her mouth. Slowing the pace, he gently brushed their lips together in a whisper-soft caress. Parting her lips again, he delved into her mouth, searching. Their tongues met as Ash deepened the kiss further.

Maddie whimpered in protest when his mouth left hers, only to moan in pleasure as he kissed a path along her jaw toward her ear. A soft gasp escaped as he lightly nipped her lobe. Ash outlined the delicate swirl of her ear, which elicited a shudder. As goose bumps broke out along her skin, his tongue gently explored the dainty contours of her ear. Maddie felt her panties dampen with her arousal.

Ash kissed his way down the side of her neck and paused to say in a voice raspy with desire, "God, sweetheart, you taste so good. Better than I imagined."

Maddie realized that one hand was grasping a fistful of his shirt, while the other was tangled in his hair and holding him to her. She leaned toward him for another kiss, but he shook his head.

"Just give me a second, sweetheart. We haven't finished our discussion and I want to be clear on things before we continue."

"Discussion?" she parroted.

Though his eyes were still dark with desire, she detected a twinkle of amusement. His lips, now slightly fuller from their kiss, lifted in a half smile. "Yeah, our discussion about whether or not we'd have this chemistry tomorrow. I'm pretty sure that won't be a problem. Hell, I don't think it will be a problem in a year. And if you don't stop looking at me like that, I'm not going to be held responsible for my actions." The last was said with a groan.

Blinking back to reality, she realized she'd been staring hungrily at his lips while he spoke. But really, they were extremely sexy. She wondered how they would feel on other parts of her.

Unknowingly, she swayed toward him.

Ash steadied her. "Maddie, did you hear what I said?"

Dragging her gaze up to his, she tried to concentrate on his last words. Wait a minute. Had he said a year? The thought acted as a douse of cold water. Well, maybe more like a mist of tepid water, but at least now her brain was functioning. "What do you mean in a year?"

"That's what I've been trying to say. I'm not interested in a casual affair. I'm looking for a relationship." His tone was exasperated, yet the look in his eyes was very, very serious.

A relationship? As in one of those things where two people were exclusive and walked down the path that could eventually lead toward — gulp — wedding bells? Ash wanted one of those? With her? Her mind couldn't quite comprehend it.

A dozen excuses immediate came to mind as to why it wouldn't work. She wasn't at a place in her life where she could work on one. There was the distance to consider. A man like Ash wouldn't be content for long with a woman like her, he was much too...potent. Sexually charged.

Whatever the word was, he had it in spades, while she, plain old Maddie Summers, did not. No, a relationship right now, especially with this man, was completely out of the question. And that small part of her that was jumping up and down yelling "Please, oh please, oh please" had just better get over it.

She tried not to hate herself as she felt forced to say, "Well, then I guess we have a problem, because right now I can't do a relationship."

Almost imperceptibly his jaws tightened. "Why not?" he inquired, in a notably cooler tone.

"Because I, uh, I don't have the time."

He merely raised a brow at that.

She agreed with his disbelieving stare. That was a ridiculous reason. But she had to make him understand. She had to convince both of them why a relationship wasn't a good idea. "Up until recently I worked two jobs so I could save more money. I'm so close to having enough in the bank, I can smell the new books on the shelves. But there's still so much I have to do to get ready. I've been working on a proposal for the bank, a business plan for myself, project expense reports and all of the rest that goes with it. I don't want anything else going on that could interfere with that."

"And a relationship would?"

"Yes," she replied. She could tell he was irritated with her pathetic excuse, but it was partially true. "Ash, I still don't think you understand—"

He cut her off with an impatient gesture. "No, I understand all too well. Right now your work comes first." The smile he gave her was full of self-derision. "Believe me when I say I've been there, done that. That's exactly why I'm not doing it anymore."

"No, that's not it either. I want to put all of my efforts into this. It's been my dream for too long for me to turn away from it now. And if I'm in a relationship, I want to be able to give one hundred and ten percent. If I'm in a relationship *and* trying to get my store going at the same time, I'll only be able to devote a fraction of my time to each." She implored him with her gaze. "Don't you see? It wouldn't be fair to me and it wouldn't be fair to the other person in the relationship." Silently she added, *and when you get tired of me, it wouldn't be fair to my heart.*

He was silent for so long she started to twist her fingers. Finally he asked, "So you're waiting on a relationship until after you get your store up and running?"

"I guess so." This had to be one of the strangest conversations she'd ever had with a man.

"How long before that'll happen?"

"Um, I'm not sure. I need to go through all the paperwork for the loan. I also need to save a little more money for padding, and then I'll sign the papers. After the loan is approved I have to order inventory, set everything up—"

"I know the process, but how *long* until you're situated?" he asked impatiently.

She chewed on her lower lip and did a few mental calculations. "Well, I suppose if all goes well, in three, maybe four months."

Ash raised a brow. "That soon?"

"Well, I already have the building, so the loan is only for the equipment, inventory and all the rest." The last thing Maddie wanted to talk about right now was the bookstore. "What does it matter?"

The slow smile he gave her made her toes curl. "It really doesn't, I was just trying to figure out my timeline. But now that that's settled, let's move on to more important things."

Settled? What in the world had they settled? First he'd told her he wanted a re…relationship—she silently stumbled over the word—and then he'd given her the third degree on her bookstore. And what had he meant by his timeline? She opened her mouth to ask that very question but he silenced her effectively with his lips.

Chapter Seven

൧

Ash had the most amazing lips. He wasted no time showing her how skillfully he knew how to use them. This was not a soft exploration of his mouth on hers. Instead his mouth was urgent and hungry. Any doubts that he desired her disappeared beneath the smoldering heat of his kiss.

His taste held a hint of wine, the right amount of masculinity and a whole lot of raw sex appeal. Sighing with pleasure, she wound her arms around his neck and moved closer. Maddie returned the kiss with equal fervor. She could feel his erection nestled against her stomach and felt a strong pull of desire at the contact.

When he broke the kiss, she grasped his head and tried to pull him back, murmuring a protest—partly because her legs had suddenly lost the ability to hold her upright, and mostly because she wasn't even close to being done with his lips.

"Sweetheart, if we keep this up, I'll embarrass myself," he rasped in a voice heavy with need. "I want to take this slow. Make it perfect for you."

Her body was thrumming with pleasure, nearly on the edge, and he wanted to take it slow? "Ash, I want you now. We can go slow next time, just please don't stop now." Her voice was tinged with desperation.

"Maddie, I need you to be sure." Though his arousal was obvious, she knew he was asking her permission to continue. She also knew if she asked him to, he'd stop. Even if it killed him and regardless of the fact she'd been the one to initiate the evening.

The tug at her heartstrings was hard to ignore in the face of his generosity. But the pounding of her heart and the excitement thrumming through her veins momentarily overrode the emotional upheaval.

She smiled beyond her desire and replied, "I've never been so sure of anything in my life." And she meant it. Before the words had left her lips, her dress was on the floor.

Ash made a strangled sound deep in his throat as he stared at her. His mouth opened a few times before any words came out. "You...ah...wow!" Not the most eloquent thing he could have said, but she had literally left him speechless.

Her generous breasts were cupped in a shimmering pink concoction of lace that was sheer enough for him to catch a peek of her lush nipples. A little lower, the same material covered just enough to tease a man unmercifully. And stockings with the barest hint of shimmer covered her long, long legs.

God almighty, her curves made his mouth water and his erection even harder. Which he hadn't thought was physically possible. She was his waking, walking wet dream come to life.

"Ash?"

Her soft inquiry startled him. With a jolt, he realized he'd been standing there gaping at her. "Maddie, sweetheart, you look sexy as hell. I don't...I just, ah, need a minute here to resume breathing."

Ash barely heard her sexy little laugh, enthralled with the way her full breasts were heaving with each breath she took. He'd always had a thing for tits, and hers were perfect. Enough to fill his hands and more. His mouth watered at the thought of sucking on the exquisite tips of her nipples until she begged for mercy. His erection throbbed painfully when he imagined pressing the plump mounds together and sliding his dick in the creamy valley. Her soft skin would feel so damn good against his cock.

Just thinking about what he could do with her tits brought him too damn close for comfort.

Maddie had moved closer during his erotic reverie. Grabbing his shirt, she tugged it over his head. "You've got too many clothes on."

He wholeheartedly agreed, but when she reached for his belt, he backed a step away. "You'd better let me do that." As much as his body craved her touch, it would be too much, too soon. Ash quickly removed the rest of his clothes, using the scant seconds to gain a small measure of control.

Now it was her turn to gape. It was incredibly arousing to see the appreciation in her eyes as she stared at him.

Going to the gym was something he did for stress relief, but he was proud to see it was now paying off in other areas of his life. He felt her fingers gently roaming over his shoulders, his chest and down his stomach.

Ash sucked in a sharp breath and grabbed them before they could go any lower. "Not yet."

"But I just want to —"

He crushed his lips to hers and carried her to the bed, effectively silencing her once more. A long moment later, he raised his head. "Next time will be for exploring. But I'm too damned worked up to last through you touching me."

Eyes that had gone from hazel to dark green stared back at him. She was barely able to nod her understanding before his fingers were stroking the skin above the waistband of her panties. Closing her eyes, she clutched at the sheets in agonized expectation.

Slowly, so very slowly, his fingers lightly traced her cleft through the damp material. The lace panties were fitted to her perfect curves as if they'd been made for her. Ash could see her dark curls behind the sheer pink and felt his gut clench with lust.

Careful to keep his touch light, he ran his finger along the waistband, skimming it along her soft stomach. When she sucked in her breath, he smiled to himself and moved to her side, curving his finger down along her hip...to her thigh...

"Mmm, I think I'm getting warmer sweetheart. What do you think?" he mused, as he once again came back to where the pink lace was hot with her moisture.

Back arched, she gasped at the soft touch. Through clenched teeth she all but growled, "Ash, you're not the only one on the edge here. Please…"

But he ignored her and let his fingers continue to torment. "So wet. Sweetheart, you are so wet for me." His husky voice was filled with awe at the discovery.

Anticipation shuddered through her as he leisurely slid a finger under the silky material. Again she waited for him to do…something, anything! And again he continued to teasingly caress. Not quite where she wanted him to be, but close. Very close.

She swallowed a cry as one long finger finally sought the wetness, the heat at the core of her.

Finally.

Unable to keep still, she moved her hips restlessly as he slid his finger inside. His other hand went to her hip, stilling the motion. Her growl of frustration died away as a second finger joined the first. His movements were slow and controlled as he tested her.

When his thumb rubbed against her clitoris, she nearly screamed with pleasure. A little faster, his fingers slid in and out while his thumb plied her most sensitive spot. He was no longer trying to still her hips as she bucked against his hand while her pleasure continued to mount.

A few seconds more was all it took for her to reach her crest. A cascade of sensations rolled through her as her body trembled with the force of the orgasm.

Before the tremors had even subsided, she was already reaching for him. It wasn't enough. Not nearly enough of what she wanted from him this night.

As soon as she was able to take a breath, she pleaded, "Ash…please. I need you."

At those magic words, he stood up and rummaged around in his slacks for the foil packet. Maddie watched him fumbling, hoping he would hurry.

Suddenly, he cursed in a low voice. "Dammit! Where in the hell is it?" Another futile search had him groaning.

Eyes filled with something akin to agony, he turned to her. "You don't happen to have a condom, do you?"

She felt like crying with frustration.

A condom? A dozen words came to mind, none of them helpful.

She knew she'd forget something this evening, but why did it have to be the most important thing? It had only been a couple of years since she'd had sex, but protection was not something a girl should forget. Especially at a crucial time like this.

This was horrible.

"Um…" She didn't know what to say. At least nothing that would make the situation more bearable.

Ash exhaled loudly, as if he'd been holding his breath. He made a sound that was half groan, half laugh. "Well, if that's not something to kill the mood. I think I would have preferred a cold shower." He raked a hand through his hair, spiking it in different directions. She watched, fascinated, as the muscles in his arms bunched with the movement.

"Maddie, I'm sorry. You have no idea just how sorry. I thought I had one, and I… Damn. I don't know how I could forget." He shook his head and looked around. "You think they'd have the rooms stocked with them or something…"

Looking around, he seemed at a loss when he realized there were none to be found.

Maddie knew he had to be hurting considering his erection was still rock-hard and huge. In her mind, there was only one solution. "Ash, we can get condoms later. Why don't you come back over here and let me…ah…" she faltered for a moment.

He stared at her intently, smiling wickedly as he grasped her intentions. "Maddie?"

"Hmm?"

"Do you...that is, would you mind if I...tried something a little different?"

A little wary, she nodded slowly in acceptance. She knew he wouldn't hurt her, what she didn't know was if she would live up to his expectations. Whatever they might be.

He dropped onto the bed and straddled her thighs. His hands skimmed behind her back to undo the clasp of her bra. Ash tossed it aside and pushed her back against the pillows. He leaned close for a kiss. "I won't hurt you," he murmured against her lips.

"I know," she returned, just as softly.

Moving lower, he took her breast in his hand. "The moment I first saw you, I wanted to taste you here." He touched his tongue to her nipple, pleased with the light flush that colored her skin.

Maddie arched against him as he drew her deep, deeper into the hot cavern of his mouth. He paid the same, loving attention to her other hardened peak, relishing the sound of her sexy moans.

Another time he'd spend hours simply feasting on her tits, but right now he had to find his own release. With his tongue, he generously moistened the valley between her breasts. Discretely spitting into his hand, he took a second to quickly lubricate his dick. All the while Maddie watched him beneath lowered lids.

Sitting up, he moved higher on her body, until he straddled her stomach.

"I love your breasts, sweetheart."

Her eyes closed with the endearment. Her breath came in short gasps when he slid his cock between the responsive peaks. Gently, he held her breasts against his throbbing flesh. The warmth of her skin made him groan with satisfaction. Maddie's soft hands came up to grasp his ass as he began to thrust.

Pumping slowly, he took care to drag his shaft along her smooth skin. Ash didn't think he'd ever get over how soft she felt. He'd been right about one thing. This was the most exquisite torture he could endure.

Ash began to move faster, squeezing her nipples as he did. The tanned skin of his hands was a sharp contrast to the pale color of her breasts. It was a sight that made his gut clench. She was so damn beautiful. And it felt so damn good to feel his cock sliding between her tits. He watched the plump flesh give with each move of his hips. He cupped his palms along the sides of her breasts, pressing them more firmly against his dick. Pure male satisfaction roared through him as he watched his erection nearly disappear between the creamy mounds. Again and again.

Three long thrusts later and he pulled back. Pumping his hand up and down his length, he spent himself on her stomach. Maddie brought her hand down to his shaft and helped to wring the last few drops from his tip.

Shuddering as the waves of his orgasm continued to roll through him, he fought for breath.

When he could finally move, he rolled off the bed to grab a washcloth. After he'd cleaned her off, he sat down beside her. She was watching him with a fascinated expression. He leaned over for a small sampling of her mouth, only because he couldn't help himself. He'd just experienced his most secret fantasy—a woman's complete and utter trust in the bedroom. She couldn't know the gift she'd given him by simply trusting him. And he definitely wanted to explore the options it opened up for them.

Ash wanted to find the words to tell her what it had meant to him.

Maddie spoke before he had the chance. "Ash, I'm really sorry."

He drew back in surprise. "Sorry? For what?"

"Well—" she dropped her gaze to his chest. "For not having a condom."

Pained laughter rumbled in his chest. He was sorry too. But only because his desire for her had not yet been sated, which is exactly what he told her.

Maddie looked up and captured his gaze, where she saw her hunger mirrored. Her eyes were then drawn down to his lips, where she saw the familiar quirk she was coming to love.

Whoa.

Love?

Where had that come from? No, she thought it was adorable. One of his many adorable habits. Wait, that didn't sound much better. If she was picking up on his habits, adorable or otherwise, that meant she was getting to know him. In a personal way. Although she wasn't aware of the rules and regulations of a brief affair, she did know that getting personal with a man was a big no-no. At least outside of the bedroom.

Honesty was a big part of her persona, so she had to admit the more time she spent with him the more she was beginning to like him. A twinge of regret reminded her of the dangers of that.

This week was about taking chances, having fun and exploring parts of herself she'd never dared to open up. Which was great for a week. When she got home, however, life would return to normal. Go to work, save every dime and put any extra hours toward the store. There was no room in that schedule for a relationship, let alone a long-distance relationship. And there was no room for the heartbreak she was sure he'd leave her with.

No matter that Ash was the most interesting, gorgeous, sexy, funny man she'd ever met. Or that he made her feel beautiful and his touch sent jolts of pleasure through her body. Or that he was an amazing kisser. Or that he thought he wanted a relationship. Or that...

A heavy sigh escaped her. Great. Just great. Her emotions had already started the descent toward the place of no return.

That certain four-letter word that made confirmed bachelors shudder and self-proclaimed feminists cringe.

Ash misunderstood her sigh and grabbed her hand. "Maddie, I'm really sorry too. I guess the timing was off. Though I have to admit what just happened was one of my biggest fantasies."

Her eyes widened, but she remained silent at his admission.

"We still have the rest of the week. I'll more than make it up to you. I'd offer to run to the gift shop and get some, but I think the damage has been done for the evening." His tone was apologetic as his fingers lightly traced her palm. He brought a hand up to cup her cheek. "Besides, this will give us a chance to get to know each other a little better. What do you say we take a few classes together and maybe go on one of the guided hikes?"

"No," she protested quickly. At his look of surprise, she realized how rude that had sounded. But didn't he realize that getting to know each other was not part of her plan? It would be a bad idea. A very bad idea. It would only allow her to find more things about him to like, things would become complicated and she'd be in a big mess. She had no intention of letting this become complicated. It was simply supposed to be two people acting on their mutual desire.

Rubbing the heels of her hands against her eyes, she had to admit it was a pretty weak excuse. But it was only a few nights they were talking about. She had already explained to Ash why she only wanted a vacation affair and he had seemed to accept that. Or had he? Frowning, she tried to remember exactly how they'd left the conversation. All she could recall was explaining her reasons to him and then kissing and then Ash had made her forget everything else.

He jolted her back from her thoughts. "So is that a no to the classes, or a no to the whole thing?" Though his tone was light, she could see the tension in his gaze.

Still frowning slightly, she replied, "I don't know. I just...I guess that depends." When he raised a brow in question, she quickly amended, "What, um, what classes were you thinking about? And are you sure—I mean really sure—that you want to spend your whole vacation with me?" Maddie really couldn't understand why he would want to. She'd seen the other women around this place. At least enough of them to know Ash could have his pick.

She wasn't certain, but she could have sworn she saw a flash of relief in his eyes before he said, "I don't know about all the classes they offer, but yes I do want to spend time with you. What's the harm in spending a little time together? It's only for a few days and I wouldn't mind the company."

If only he knew how much harm had already been done. A few more days and she'd fall completely head over heels. However, when she thought about the alternative of spending the time alone—or even worse—in the company of someone like Cole Hawthorn, she knew she'd much rather be with Ash. With no small amount of trepidation, she finally agreed. "Yeah, okay. I have one condition, though."

"What's that?"

"We have to do at least one yoga class." She wanted to know she had control over one aspect of this vacation, however small.

"Yoga?" Ash looked as if he'd swallowed something foul. "Where they expect you to twist and contort your body into impossible positions?"

Maddie had to laugh at his expression. "It's not that bad. I even bet you'll feel better afterward. So, do we have a deal?"

"Uh, sure." The doubt in his voice was almost comical. Their eyes met and they both smiled. His gaze dropped and his smile vanished. Looking down, Maddie realized Ash was staring intently at her nearly nude body. She quickly covered herself, but it was too late.

Desire flared between them once again.

His features were tight when he stood stiffly to gather the rest of his clothes. "It's late. I'd better get going." Once his slightly rumpled clothes were on, he turned to her. "I do know there's a spinning class at 8:30 tomorrow morning if you're interested."

"Great," she said with forced enthusiasm.

"Okay then. I'll...uh...just let myself out. Don't forget to lock the door after me."

Then he was gone, the door shutting softly behind him. Maddie fell back onto the bed with a groan. She didn't know whether to laugh or cry. Some seductress she was. She had been so wrapped up in thoughts of seducing him, she'd forgotten about protection. Because of her glaring oversight, she now only had four more nights to be with Ash.

Wrapping the sheet around her, she went over to lock the door like he'd said. As awkward as that had been, he'd still been thoughtful enough to be concerned about her safety.

Most men would have been more anxious to get out the door than worry if she was going to lock it behind them. Maddie had quickly learned that Ash was definitely not like most men.

Therein lay the crux of the problem.

When she'd first met him, he'd looked like a playboy who gave new meaning to the word debauchery with his dark good looks. Which would have made him the perfect man to seduce. What Maddie hadn't counted on was his witty charm or sense of humor. Things that made a woman think in more permanent terms. Even at a place like this.

Ugh. Her thoughts were beginning to sound like a broken record. She'd made up her mind to have a vacation fling and that's exactly what she'd do. Returning to the bed, she lay back down.

Alone.

Her hypersensitive body was still reeling from his touch. It was going to happen tomorrow night. Closing her eyes, she imagined what it would be like when they finally came together. It would be a mind-blowing experience for the both of them. Fantastic sex. No more, no less. And when she went home she'd be able to look back and smile about the whole thing with no regrets. No regrets at all. And that's exactly what she'd keep telling herself.

* * * * *

By the time Ash stepped back into his own room, he was once again as hard as a rock. And more frustrated than he'd ever been. What kind of idiot forgets a condom? Wouldn't you know, when he finally meets *the one*, he forgets. Of course, one wouldn't have been near enough for the long evening he'd had planned, but it would have been a hell of a lot better than none at all. Had he remembered to get one in the first place, he probably would have had the foresight to get a few extra. Even more pathetic was the fact that they were at an erotic resort.

Damn. He could kick his own ass right about now. Though he'd found release, he was still wound tight. Ash wanted nothing more than to bury himself inside her. He wanted that connection with her.

Frowning in thought, he figured he'd at least have to make a suggestion to the staff to put complimentary condoms in each room. No chocolates on the pillows here. Ash shook his head in disgust.

When Maddie had come apart in his arms, it had been the most beautiful sight he had ever seen. And he had wanted — still wanted — to watch her do it all over again.

Muttering under his breath, he stripped down and turned the shower on.

Cold.

He gritted his teeth against the icy spray hitting his skin. Though it did little to fix his immediate problem, it did help to clear his head enough for rational thought.

As much as he hated to admit it, it was probably better the evening had been interrupted. Maddie was too good for a quick roll in the sack. Much too good. Hell, she was too good for the treatment she'd already received at his hands. But he'd been unable to help himself.

She was the kind of woman who deserved to be thoroughly romanced. Slowly savored. Ash wanted this to be so much more than a casual night of sex. Then again, a long, drawn-out romance wasn't going to work either.

If things worked out the way he wanted, he'd have the rest of their lives to make love to her. Right now it was much more important he convince her why they both deserved more than a vacation fling. After tonight he was even more certain she was the one.

He knew she wasn't after his money. With a grimace, he had to admit that she was currently only after his body. Which was definitely flattering, but still not enough.

Never one to settle for less than everything, he already had plans for her to be wearing the ring, dress and sexy little garter belt while floating down the aisle in no more than six months. The tough part was going to be letting her in on his plans. Not to mention getting around her obvious reservations. He couldn't help but admire her determination to get her bookstore up and running as soon as possible. He couldn't count how many times he'd put his personal life on hold for important business matters, and this was important to her. What he needed was a way to make her understand she could still have her dream *and* a relationship at the same time.

There was no way he was going to let her walk away.

Ash didn't believe in coincidence, and their meeting here had been no coincidence. Call it destiny or fate or even luck, he wasn't going to question his good fortune. He'd come here to check out a possible investment, as well as take a few days and figure out what to do with the rest of his life. And Maddie was it. He still hadn't made up his mind about the resort, though.

Stepping out of the shower, he toweled off and lay down on the bed. He had four days left. Four days to persuade her that a relationship, a permanent relationship between them, would be perfect.

A confident smile drew his lips up at the corners. He'd never failed before, and there was no way in hell he was going to fail when the most important thing in his life was at stake.

Love.

Turning onto his side, he began working on a business plan for Erect Correct Briefs. The effects of the cold shower had worn off much too quickly, and knowing Maddie was only a door away was wreaking havoc on his already rebellious libido. Tomorrow he'd go to the gift and novelty shop and buy a bagful of condoms. Enough that he could put one in every pocket.

Make that three in every pocket.

Somewhere between midnight and two o'clock in the morning, Ash finally managed to fall asleep. He escaped his waking thoughts of Maddie, only to dream of her.

She was lying on his bed, her silken limbs awaiting his touch. Indulging his curiosity, he leisurely worked his way down her body, taking his sweet time to taste every luscious inch of her. And yes, she tasted delicious. Exactly as he remembered she did.

A nibble at her neck. A long, slow lick along the underside of her breast up to the tip of her nipple. He took a moment to feast on the perfect tip. Suckling hard, he reveled in her moan of ecstasy. Pressing kisses along her skin, he made his way to the other breast, lavishing the same devout attention to her other perfect nipple. Her fingers were clenched in his hair. Her sweet cries urged him on. He knew he'd never get over this particular craving.

He pressed one last soft kiss to the pert tip and then licked his way down her stomach. Stopping to taste her navel...the delicious curve of her hip...

She writhed under him, begging and pleading, though he wasn't sure if she wanted him to stop or continue with the sensual torture. The insistent throb of his erection decided for him. Reaching for the condom, he slid it on and prepared to enter her warmth when he realized he couldn't.

The condom had turned into a pair of constrictive briefs. No matter how hard he tried to maneuver himself, his erection could not be freed. Maddie was staring at him with hunger and regret while he tried to explain. And the more he tried to explain, the more constrictive the briefs became, until he was sure the pressure had cut off vital blood flow.

Ash woke in a cold sweat. The pressure from his raging erection had faded to something a tad less raging and a lot more...limp.

What had started out as an erotic fantasy had quickly turned into a nightmare. Damned if he hadn't been done in by his own brilliant invention. At the moment, his so-called brilliant invention didn't seem all that appealing.

Chapter Eight

છ

After a long night spent tossing and turning, Maddie woke frustrated. The memory of Ash's touch had kept her burning with need. And cursing her forgetfulness. She'd been seriously tempted to call room service and order the "Midnight Fantasy". The package included a vibrator, warming oil and dark chocolate for afterward. The waiter was optional. It had sounded better than the Bucket O' Bondage or the Tongue Teaser.

In the end, it hadn't been Ash, so she'd skipped it. Instead, she'd fallen asleep wondering with an idle curiosity if the Dangling Duo could really do everything the brochure promised.

She decided to forgo a shower since she was going to get hot and sweaty in the spinning class, but she did want to look good. Or as good as she could with no shower, makeup or fixing her hair. Pulling out a fitted tank and matching exercise shorts, she surveyed herself critically in the mirror after putting them on.

The pink and charcoal gray ensemble was cute in a flirty sort of way. And it covered enough of her that she felt comfortable wearing it. This had been another Kris-inspired impulse buy. Maddie was much more comfortable in a baggy T-shirt and sweats when working out, rather than a skimpy outfit. On her, those tended to show more jiggle and bounce than muscle tone and definition.

Definitely not something she wanted to wear when trying to impress a guy like Ash.

Giving her hair one last pat, she was soon ready to go. The butterflies in her stomach would not relax, however. She wasn't quite sure how to face Ash this morning after the way they'd left things. What was she supposed to say? "Good morning, Ash. I hope you slept well after we almost had sex."

Rolling her eyes, she rummaged around in her suitcase for a pack of gum. She figured she at least owed him fresh breath. Thankfully the spinning class would help to burn off some excess energy—also known as lust—and get her mind on other things. Plus, there wouldn't be much time or breath for talking.

After pulling almost everything out of her suitcase, she finally managed to locate the gum. It was right on top of a box of—oh no—a big box of condoms!

Shocked, Maddie picked it up. Where in the world had this come from? Then she noticed the small note attached. It read, *Maddie, I hope this comes in handy with all the sexy guys you're going to meet. Love, Kris.*

This box had been in her luggage the whole time. She dropped onto the bed and laughed until tears rolled down her cheeks. Or maybe the laughter had turned into tears.

Either way she couldn't believe it.

Ash knocked on the door and was surprised to see a sobbing Maddie open it. "Hey, what's wrong?"

She just shook her head and held up a box. He ignored it for a moment and took her arm. "Are you okay? What happened?"

The muffled noise she was making sounded suspiciously like laughter. He looked at the box to see if it would provide him with a clue. The concern on his face quickly turned to disbelief.

His eyebrows rose as he stared at a large box of condoms. He was flattered and at the same time intimidated by her assumptions about his stamina. When he'd said he had the stamina of a stallion, he'd been kidding. Mostly. "Uh, does this mean you want to have dinner tonight?"

Still laughing, she managed to splutter, "N-no...I found...this...in m-my suitcase."

"Your suitcase?" His brows drew down as her words sunk in. "Are you telling me you had this here the whole time?"

"Y-yes!" Her shoulders still shook, but he wasn't sure now if it was with laughter. Hell, he didn't know whether to laugh or curse himself. Although she wouldn't meet his gaze, he could see faint circles under her eyes. Obviously her night hadn't been much better than his. He could only hope her dreams had been better. The whole time that box had been sitting there.

Mocking them.

"Why didn't you say something?"

"I didn't know it was there! My friend helped me pack and she must have snuck it in when I wasn't looking. I just found it this morning." The last was said with such obvious remorse, Ash suddenly felt like smiling.

It would definitely be tonight.

Tonight he'd make love to Maddie. The way he was feeling, he bet he could make a sizeable dent in that box. First they had to get through the day, and their spinning class started in less than fifteen minutes.

He took hold of her arm and steered her out the door. "Don't worry sweetheart, we'll get to them tonight."

"I'll hold you to that," she grumbled, but he noticed a little color lit her cheeks and her lips lifted in a small smile.

My sweet and sassy Maddie is lurking in there somewhere, he thought with amusement.

* * * * *

They got to the class on time and Maddie selected two bikes while Ash grabbed a couple bottles of water. The room had about fifteen bikes and only eight of them were currently taken. Maybe it was a little too early for the spa goers. Truth be told, it was a little too early for her.

She was surprised and relieved to see perky Shannon walk into the room and introduce herself as the instructor.

Good. A familiar face to help start the day off right.

Shannon took her place at the front of the class, settling onto her bike. Everything went downhill from there.

"Good morning everyone! Glad you could make it to our topless spinning class."

Maddie looked around as Shannon and the rest of the class removed their tops.

Great.

Glaring at Ash, she was slightly mollified to note he seemed as surprised as she was. He gave her a shrug and offered an apology. Then ruined the effect by taking his shirt off and looking at her expectantly.

"No way," she muttered. Lowering her gaze to the bike, she studiously ignored the sea of nipples and focused on the many ways she would torture Ash for this.

Fifteen minutes into the class, she was beginning to think the perky attitude Shannon adopted was really a façade that hid an evil fitness demon. Though it wasn't the first spinning class Maddie had attended, it was definitely the most challenging. In a brutal, sweaty, won't-be-able-to-move-tomorrow sort of way. Ash definitely deserved to pay for this.

The pace was much too fast to allow for conversation, so Maddie dutifully pedaled beside him, plotting her revenge. Shannon continued to push them on.

And on, and on, and on.

An eternity or maybe it was only an hour later, Shannon, whom Maddie had unflatteringly dubbed the Spinning Shrew, allowed them to cool down. When it came time to leave, she was barely able to drag herself off the bike. Exhaustion helped to dull the sight of all the bared breasts and quivering thighs surrounding her.

Of course Ash stood there looking too darn attractive with his flushed cheeks and the light sheen of sweat covering his body. Even as tired as she was, her body was still able to muster a flicker of desire. It could have been more than a flicker, but her muscles were almost numb so she wasn't sure.

It wasn't fair that he could look so…yummy after that. She knew her cheeks were bright red from exertion and chunks of hair had escaped her ponytail. They were currently plastered to her neck, compliments of the buckets of sweat she'd produced. The effect couldn't be attractive.

While Maddie continued to mull over her appearance, Ash was thinking about how sexy she looked. He found Maddie's pink cheeks and lopsided ponytail very appealing. After they made love, he suspected her cheeks would have the same enticing glow and instead of a ponytail, her hair would be loose and spread across the pillow.

His pillow.

They would both be damp with sweat after their marathon session of hot, sweaty —

Her voice broke into his fantasy. "Well, now that I'm looking my best, what do you say we go grab something to eat? I'm starving."

Ash picked up on the self-mocking note in her voice and frowned. Was it possible that she didn't know her own appeal? Or was she simply fishing for a compliment? No, this was Maddie, who seemed about as calculating as a newborn babe compared to the women he'd escaped.

Frank admiration lit his gaze as he replied honestly, "I think you look pretty damn good right now."

"Oh, absolutely. And after breakfast, I think I'll go enter myself into a beauty contest," she laughed. "I'm sure I'll be nominated for Best Hair." She punctuated the statement with an exaggerated flip of her hair and batting of her eyelashes. "I'd try for the Best Boobs competition, but considering how a few of those ladies managed not to jiggle and bounce throughout the class, I don't think I'd have a chance."

They'd been headed in the direction of the dining room, but he stopped her. Moving her off to the side, he tipped her chin and searched her eyes, which flickered with uncertainty. Amazing.

She really had no idea. Maddie was a walking puzzle. One minute she was planning to seduce him and the next she was blushing with innocence and denying her own beauty.

He had the impression she would shrug off any compliments he could give her. So instead, he opted for the truth. "Sweetheart, I'll be the first to admit that not everybody looks good after a workout. But you do. In fact, I was just imagining you're cheeks would have the same sweet blush right after we make love. And I'm hoping I'll be able to make you just as tired."

There. The comment had produced a small smile.

He brushed his thumb across her full bottom lip. It would be so easy to lean over for a taste. Her small pink tongue darted out to lick her lips. Ash stifled his groan. The woman was more tempting than Helen of Troy any day. Especially in the little exercise outfit she had on. It was modest compared to what most of the women had worn—or hadn't worn—but he knew what it concealed. And the knowledge drove him crazy like nothing else could have.

Remembering they were in public, he forced his gaze elsewhere. "You were beautiful last night in that dress, and you're beautiful this morning. And your breasts are perfect." The tentative smile turned into a radiant grin, which nearly turned his heart over.

Beautiful had been an understatement. This woman was a knockout.

"You really mean it, don't you?"

He returned her smile. "Yeah, I do." But it was time to change the subject, for his hunger wasn't for food at the moment and it was becoming difficult to remember that she needed to eat. "Now how about some breakfast? All this talk about your beauty is giving me an appetite."

In a flash, the uncertainty was gone, replaced with mischief. "Craving oysters? Isn't it a little early in the day for seafood?"

"You're never going to let me live that one down, are you?" he asked ruefully.

"Not a chance." She twined her arm through his. "Let's go feed you, oh great stallion."

Groaning, he allowed her to pull him away. Just his luck that she possessed beauty and a perfect memory. On the other hand, she was teasing him as if they were close.

Perfect.

They each ate a hearty breakfast, minus any melon body parts, and sat back to savor a steaming cup of coffee. Maddie took a sip of the reviving brew and sighed with appreciation. Ash watched her over the rim of his cup, marveling at her obvious enjoyment. He couldn't remember the last time he'd sat down and simply enjoyed a cup of coffee.

Until two days ago, his life had been filled with...nothing. It had been completely empty. Empty of the simple pleasures in life, empty of genuine smiles and sincere compliments, at least from the women of his acquaintance. But most of all, it had been empty without Maddie. She was forcing him to see exactly what he'd been missing out on all this time.

Not wanting to dwell on that train of thought, he pushed it from his mind. Instead he gave her a devilish grin and said, "Are you going to be up for that hike this afternoon?"

She pretended to ponder the question. "I guess that depends on whether or not you want to carry me most of the way."

"Works for me," he quipped, waggling his eyebrows suggestively.

Maddie rolled her eyes. More seriously, she said, "I think I could handle it after a hot shower and a nap."

"Great. It's not until 1:30 this afternoon. And it's actually more of a guided walk than a strenuous hike, so it shouldn't be too bad."

She inhaled deeply and wrinkled her nose. The unmistakable odor of her own person had her saying, "I don't know about you, but I need a shower."

Unbidden images of what they could do in a shower leapt into his mind. Unfortunately, she had a point. He didn't smell all that sweet either.

He left her at her door with a quick brush of his lips. "I'll see you this afternoon." Heading back to his own room, he resigned himself to another long, cold shower. Despite his body's need to have her, he didn't want to rush things any more than he already had. They both needed this chance to get to know one another.

Maddie, on the other hand, enjoyed a blissfully hot shower, which helped to ease the tightness in her muscles. With regret, she eventually turned the water off and stepped out. Shuffling through her clothes, she spied the box of condoms. One more thing she owed Kris for.

The box was fairly large and Maddie wondered at Kris' optimism on her behalf. Opening it, she could only shake her head in amusement. Not only were there plenty of condoms, but there was also a small bottle of strawberry-flavored warming liquid, a red feather, and a pair of edible panties, also strawberry flavored. All of which promised an erotically good time.

My, oh my.

As much as she appreciated the gesture, she didn't think she'd need any extra toys with Ash. The man could heat her with a simple look.

A soft laugh escaped as she imagined Kris sneaking the box into her luggage. She was truthfully glad she hadn't known it was in there, because she would have been mortified to have the airline baggage checker rummage around and see it.

As rash as she was acting now, it was really only a role she was playing. She wasn't sure if it was the atmosphere of the place, or the fact Ash brought out her sensuality. Probably a little of both. Either way, it was only temporary. It had to be.

The shower had revived her enough that she didn't think a nap was necessary, but she still had a couple hours to waste. Looking outside, she saw the sun was out and a light breeze was wafting through the garden. The perfect reading conditions.

Maddie grabbed a novel out of her bag and headed for the gazebo she'd spotted by the hot tub.

The gazebo housed a few chairs and a porch swing. She opted for the swing, and soon immersed herself in a lighthearted comedy. Something to give her a reprieve from the sexual tension.

It was how Ash found her some time later. He stood and watched her for a few minutes, enjoying the sound of her musical laughter. Whatever she was reading had brought tears of laughter to her eyes, making them shimmer. She was curled on the swing and looked as cozy as a person could get. Ash had the overwhelming urge to kiss her.

But once again time was against them. Instead he merely stepped into view with a soft, "Hey there."

He watched her eyes widen and she scrambled off the swing. "Oh no! Don't tell me I'm late for the hike."

"No. I just came by a little early to see if you wanted to grab a bite before we take off."

She squinted at her watch and said ruefully, "Good idea. I have a tendency to forget meals when I'm reading a good book."

"I can relate, except I hardly have time to read a book, good or otherwise. I get busy with the paperwork that grows on my desk." He took her hand as they walked back to her room to drop off the book, glad when she didn't try to pull away.

"And I thought I was a workaholic," she laughed. "I always try to make a little time to read or do something relaxing. It helps keep me somewhat sane."

Ash smiled vaguely, but made no comment. He was making time for something now. Some*one*, that is.

After eating a quick meal, they went back to the bungalow so Maddie could change her shoes and slather on sunscreen. To his delight, she asked him to do the back of her neck. It was a sorry man who jumped at the chance to apply sunscreen to a woman's neck, but he was desperate. There was something sexy about the wispy hairs at the nape of her neck. Barely stopping himself from caressing the delicate area, he had a sinking feeling it was going to be a long afternoon.

Finally ready, they went to the path where they'd walked yesterday morning. A small group was milling around while the staff guide handed out hip packs. Inside they found an energy bar, a bottle of water, and a small pamphlet describing the local flora and fauna.

"What a neat idea," Maddie murmured, as she inspected the contents of the pack. When she found a condom tucked discreetly in the back, she merely raised an eyebrow. If this kept up, she'd grow immune to random sexual acts in public.

Five minutes later the guide briefly introduced himself and soon they were on their way. Ash purposely kept toward the back of the group, hoping he could have Maddie to himself. He was frustrated when he heard a suave voice say, "Maddie, hi. I was hoping I'd run into you again."

Ash felt his face freeze as he turned and saw the jerk from yesterday. The possessive feeling that surged through him was almost surprising in its intensity. Then again, all the feelings Maddie provoked in him were intense. Damned if he was going to share her today, especially with this wannabe Don Juan.

Before he could deliver a curt dismissal, Maddie replied, "Oh, hi Cole. Great day for a walk, isn't it?"

"Especially with such a beautiful lady," Cole said, with an exaggerated wink. Ash wanted to temporarily close that eye with a well-placed fist. Was this guy a moron? He thought he'd been pretty clear about staking his claim, but maybe he needed to remind Rico Suave.

Placing an arm around her waist, he pulled Maddie closer. He almost made them both trip, but luckily managed to make it look as if he was pulling her close for a kiss. Taking advantage of the opportunity, he gave her a deep kiss before releasing her.

Before she could wrench herself out of his grasp, he took her hand.

Throwing a careless grin at the other man, he said, "We decided since we were here we should try to see a little more of the place than just the walls of our room. But like you said, she's a beautiful lady. I just can't help myself." Wasn't that the truth.

Maddie's outraged gasp and pink cheeks would seem to be those of a blushing lover. Only Ash saw the fury burning in the depths of her gaze. Her blush had nothing to do with embarrassment and everything to do with anger at his comments.

A twinge of remorse swept through him, but he shrugged it off. He couldn't say he liked this possessiveness any more than she did, but right now he really couldn't seem to help himself.

"Ash! How dare you—" she seethed, but Cole was already making his escape.

"Ah, I was going to ask if you were willing to share or at least let me watch, but I can see not. It was good to see you again, Maddie." And with a terse nod in Ash's direction, Cole walked away. Ash watched him sidle up next to a group of women and start chatting amiably. Romeo obviously wasn't going to waste precious time mooning over this lost conquest. Which was good, because all he wanted to do was beat the hell out of him. Share? Let him watch!? The guy had a pair of big ones to ask something like that.

A sharp tug on his arm brought his head around to Maddie. Uh-oh. The look in her eyes was not promising.

"What was that all about? I'm surprised you didn't lift your leg and pee on me to mark your territory!"

Chagrined, he held up his hands in defense. "I'm sorry, I'm sorry. I know that was a little out of line—"

"A little out of line? Buddy, you were more than a little out of line. That was completely over the top. You made it sound as if I were some sex-starved maniac who can't keep her hands off you." Her voice had risen with each word and they were attracting a few stares. Some curious, others appraising. Noticing the attention, she dropped her voice to a harsh whisper. "You're acting like a jealous boyfriend or something."

That was exactly how he felt, but the look on her face stopped him from agreeing. She was dead set on keeping things casual between them. Now wasn't the time or place to tell her that wasn't going to happen. So he settled for saying, "I know, and I said I'm sorry. But I didn't want to share you with him, *despite* his intentions. I just said the first thing that popped into my head. Obviously it wasn't the best thing to say."

"Obviously," she muttered.

"Besides, I made *myself* sound like a sex-starved maniac. And considering where we are, that's a good thing." He quickly rushed on when she opened her mouth to argue. "Either way, I'm sorry. Will you forgive me? I'll make it up to you somehow." Thoughts of how he could pleasure her until she screamed seemed like a good way to atone for his sin.

She thought about it for a moment and sighed. "Okay, but no more of this beating your chest stuff. I'm pretty sure that went out of style along with wearing animal skins and hunting the wooly mammoth."

"Does that mean you wouldn't appreciate it if I were to drag you off by your hair?" Ash joked.

"Ha, ha. Let's keep walking, caveman."

For the next forty-five minutes, the guide entertained them with brief stories about the area and local wildlife. Some of the group members began to ask questions, while others sidled off to engage in their own communion with nature.

Ash turned to Maddie, using the opportunity to talk. "So why a bookstore?"

"What?" Taken off-guard by the question, she turned to him and blinked.

"What makes you want to open a bookstore?"

"Oh, well..." she bit her lip in indecision. He watched her hands play with the zipper on the hip pack she wore as she said in a soft voice, "Actually, it was my grandfather's dream."

Ash prodded her with an encouraging look.

"When I was little, I remember sitting on his lap and reading the most wonderful stories. Fairy tales, adventures in far-off places. You name it, and we read it. He was illiterate most of his life. In fact, he didn't learn to read until well into his late forties. To him, books were a future. He always believed if a person knew how to read, they could accomplish anything. With a book you could travel to different countries and different eras. You could meet new people and learn new things."

Ash watched the bittersweet expression on her face as she went on.

"He had always been ashamed of not knowing how to read. And when he finally learned, you always saw him with a book in front of his face."

She laughed lightly. "He read everything he could get his hands on. Mysteries, biographies, travel magazines, cookbooks...even romance novels. I can't remember a time when he wasn't trying to read something to me, or lending me a book about this or that. I always thought he was the smartest man I knew..." she trailed off with a wistful note in her voice.

"He sounds like a great man," he observed quietly.

Her smile was immediate. "The very best."

"You're lucky you were able to know him. Because my parents had me at such a late age, I never knew my grandparents."

"Yeah, I was lucky." Her smile now held a trace of sadness.

"Did he raise you?" Ash inquired.

"For the most part. I went to live with him when I was six."

"Are your parents..." he trailed off, not wanting to pry.

She shook her head. "It's okay. They were in a car crash. Some new sports car my dad had just bought and they were driving too fast. It was a long time ago. I don't have many memories of them. My grandfather died about four years ago."

When he heard the slight catch in her voice, he wrapped an arm around her. Pulling her close for a brief hug, he murmured into her hair, "Ah sweetheart, I'm really sorry to hear that."

"Thanks." Maddie returned his hug. Her eyes were suspiciously bright when she pulled away. "Anyhow, to make a long story short, I wanted something to remember my grandfather by. A tribute, I guess you could say. He'd always been there for me. As a grandfather figure, father figure, mentor. He passed on his love of reading to me so I figured, why not open a bookstore?"

"Sounds like the perfect reason to me."

During the talk they hadn't kept pace with the group and were some steps behind. He took advantage of the semi-privacy and stopped her. Taking her face between both of his hands, he slowly lowered his mouth to hers. The kiss was slow and deep. He savored the taste of her — warm, sweet and utterly feminine. With his tongue he traced the contours of her mouth, groaning when she did the same. His hand slid under her top, brushing across her nipples until they peaked. She murmured her encouragement. As he continued to feel, her hand went to the front of his shorts to brazenly cup his erection. He pushed against her palm, unable to help himself.

Ash backed her against a tree and settled her firmly between his thighs, her hand caught between them. Even then, he could feel the heat of her. The temptation was killing him.

Maddie must have felt the same, because she whispered his name and began to rub against him. He squeezed her nipple lightly, eliciting a moan of pleasure. Her hand slid under his waistband and grasped him firmly.

Ash forgot how to breathe. Her hand was stroking his dick in a rhythm so perfect he was seconds away from exploding. Every few strokes, she'd stop and use her fingers to tease the underside of his shaft and the tip of his penis. Those intermittent soft caresses were nearly his undoing.

Pushing her more firmly against the tree, he devoured her mouth, praying he'd have the courage to stop her before it was too late. Half hoping she would continue anyway.

He fingered the hem of her shirt, pulling it up just enough to put his mouth on her breast. Grazing his teeth lightly along the smooth skin, he nipped and savored to his heart's content. His tongue followed, laving her hardened nipple. Drawing the sweet peak into his mouth, he sucked hard, causing her to grasp his shaft tighter. A harsh breath hissed between his teeth at the pleasure-pain she caused.

"Maddie," he growled. "You have to stop, sweetheart. I'm too close."

Scant seconds later, they broke apart when voices from the group drew near. Ash held her to him when she would have pulled away. Not quite willing to let her go, he forced her to look at him. "Looks like the group is heading back." His voice was rough and slightly unsteady from their encounter. He blew out a breath, futilely wishing they were alone.

The smile she bestowed on him was one of delicious promise.

Ash gently brushed a stray hair behind her ear as she also tried to catch her breath. "Very, very soon, we'll finish that thought," he whispered to her.

When they were finally able to walk again, they followed the group at a more leisurely pace. Once again, they came upon the overly amorous couple, who were taking advantage of the nearest inanimate object. The man had his lover bent over a large rock and was getting ready to enter her from behind. This time Maddie didn't even blink. She was only surprised they'd made it this far on the hike.

Chapter Nine

✌

Maddie couldn't figure Ash out. One minute he was a sensual lover, the next a humorous companion, and then an understanding friend. Oh, and she couldn't forget the possessive boyfriend act he'd performed earlier. She still wasn't sure whether to be flattered or angry. Well, she could admit to a little of both. Okay, maybe a whole lot of the former, but she'd never admit it out loud.

She couldn't recall a time when two men had wanted her at the same time. Granted, the group of women Cole had insinuated himself with seemed to have effectively taken his mind off her. However, Ash had looked ready to physically remove him from her presence. Could his possessive streak mean he really *was* interested in her? Or did he just not want to share her until their fling was over?

Her thoughts came to a screeching halt. It didn't matter if he was more than a little interested in her. This was only a vacation affair. Nothing more.

By the time they got back to the resort, it was about 3:30 and Maddie was more than ready for a nap. Between the spinning class, hike and her current frame of mind, she wasn't sure if sex was a great idea at the moment.

She hadn't said anything to Ash, but the muscles in her legs were beginning to protest every little step she took. Hopefully a nice hot bath in the jetted tub would help. Even if it didn't, a relaxing bath would do wonders for her troubled mind.

He must have sensed her withdrawal, because he left her at her door with nothing more than a sweet kiss. They agreed to meet at 6:00 for dinner.

"This time it's my treat," Ash assured her, with a look that promised much more than a great meal. She slumped back against the door after it had closed behind him. As much as she didn't want to move, she was afraid her muscles would stiffen beyond the point of moving if she didn't.

Gingerly stepping out of her clothes, she leaned against the wall for support. Oh boy, this was not good. She managed to get the hot water flowing in the tub without too much trouble. By the time she settled into the tub, she'd done enough moaning and groaning to make herself blush. Anyone listening would have thought she was in the throes of a passionate encounter rather than experiencing a painful muscle spasm. Hopefully Ash hadn't heard. He might think she'd started without him.

She could barely muster the energy to smile at her own pitiful humor. Yes, tomorrow she would definitely be paying for her exercise excess of today.

She let her mind wind down while the soothing scent of the bath oil she'd added to the water, along with the jets, lulled her into a semi-conscious state. Although her stiff muscles wouldn't allow her to completely relax, she was able to enjoy the bath. It was a treat she rarely allowed herself. Not because she didn't like them, but because she seldom had the time. Actually, it was because she didn't make the time. That and the fact luxuries ultimately cost precious dollars she didn't want to spend.

This vacation was helping her to realize spending money on an occasional treat wasn't necessarily a bad thing. In fact, a massage or manicure might help to perk her up every now and then. Wouldn't Kris be amazed to hear her admit to that? She would probably think hell had frozen over.

The water had cooled considerably by the time she could rouse herself enough to step out. She barely had the energy to drag herself over to the bed. She set the alarm for five o'clock and promptly fell asleep. Her body and mind were completely exhausted.

When the alarm eventually went off, she woke feeling a bit more human. She went to swing her legs off the bed and nearly cried with the effort. The bath had done little to help her muscles. They were silently shrieking their objection to any movement she made.

"Okay, think Maddie," she said aloud. She had no desire to see another night with Ash come to a premature halt. A few tight muscles were nothing compared to her sexual frustration.

Painfully making her way over to the tub, she ran another bath. After a fifteen-minute soak, she carefully stepped out and tried to do a few gentle stretches. The pain had reduced to a dull throb, but she still wouldn't be up for any bedroom antics tonight. At least not the kind she'd been planning.

Cursing her luck, she gingerly sat down in a chair and dropped her head in her hands. Could this be a sign? Maybe she and Ash weren't meant to sleep together. She hated to believe that when her body and her heart felt it was right.

Straightening with a groan, she decided to continue on her course. She'd made a decision and she planned to stick with it. Every painful step of the way. Ash was worth it and so was she. With renewed resolve, she went about the painstaking task of getting ready for their date.

* * * * *

Ash knocked on Maddie's door feeling much more comfortable than he had the previous night. He was a man who knew his mind and his mind was on her.

Overwhelmed with thoughts of her, to be exact.

When she opened the door, his mouth went dry at the stunning picture she presented. Tonight she was dressed in a blue silk halter top that bared a good portion of her elegant back. The matching pants were slim and fitted, accentuating her long legs. A pair of high-heeled sandals showed off her sexy ankles and completed the look.

Resisting the urge to whistle, he took her hand and pressed a light kiss along the inside of her wrist. "Sweetheart, I didn't think it was possible, but you look even more beautiful tonight."

"I, um—" she stopped when he placed a finger on her lips.

"Just say 'Thank you Ash'," he instructed.

"Thank you, Ash," she repeated with a small smile.

"We have reservations awaiting us. Shall we?" He gestured grandly with his arm.

"Which restaurant are we going to?"

"The nicer of the two. It's actually been written up a few times in various travel magazines for the unusual cuisine."

"I can imagine," she replied dryly.

Laughing, he shook his head. "No. It's not what you think." Ash thought about it for a moment. "Okay, it probably is, but they really do serve excellent meals here. Very upscale."

"You're not going to expect me to eat caviar and escargot, are you?" she wrinkled her nose at the thought.

With a serious expression, he said, "I suppose not. But I hope you'll at least try some oysters with me."

"Not on your life, bud. I've tried one before and vowed never again. Once was more than enough," Maddie laughed.

His shocked expression was so exaggerated it prompted another laugh from her. "Say it isn't so! Oysters are the staple of any good diet. At least for a sex-starved maniac like myself." He clutched his chest as if in pain.

She rolled her eyes. "Now that's just plain disgusting."

"What, the oysters, or the sex-starved maniac part?"

The look she gave him was full of exasperation.

He finally cracked a smile. "Okay, I confess, oysters aren't one of my favorites either. I've never seen the appeal in swallowing something that slimy. And caviar is foul stuff." He gave a mock shudder. "I much prefer lobster or salmon."

When they arrived at the restaurant they were promptly ushered into a private booth. Soft candlelight and warm colors helped to set the mood. Almost immediately the server brought a bottle of wine and a basket of warm rolls.

Ash caught Maddie's smile. "What?"

"You said we had reservations, but you forgot to mention you ordered ahead and reserved a private booth. It's very romantic."

Flashing a sexy grin, he didn't bother to deny it. "I didn't order ahead, I just made sure they had wine ready for us. As for the private booth...well, what can I say? I want you all to myself." He watched her take a small sip of wine, and did the same.

The server came back to take their orders and then they were once again alone. Ash considered her for a moment, then said, "You know, you've told me about your family and work, but I still don't know where you're from."

Looking like a deer caught in headlights, she chewed on her lower lip. "Umm...Washington," she said finally.

He whistled softly between his teeth. "Wow. That's quite a bit of acreage you have." And if that wasn't an evasive answer, he didn't know what was. She was still leery about letting him in.

Interesting.

She laughed nervously. "Sorry. I live in Seattle."

"Hmm. I've been there a time or two on business. Never had much time to explore, but it seemed like a neat place."

"Yeah, it is a nice place. I wouldn't want to be anywhere else. What about you?"

"Right now my address is in Chicago, but I have to travel for work quite a bit, so I'm not there much."

"It doesn't sound like you consider Chicago much of a home."

He took a sip of wine before replying simply, "I don't."

She toyed with the stem of her glass. "I know how you feel. Before I bought my house, I lived in an apartment that served my basic functions of eating and sleeping. But I hated it there. I never felt comfortable enough to make it my home."

"I think my problem is that I have nothing to come home to. Just some uncomfortable furniture my decorator assured me was stylish, and whatever I haven't thrown out in my fridge."

He saw a flash of pity and something else in her eyes before she said, "So why don't you move? Or change something so you feel good about going home at the end of the day."

"Believe me, I'm working on it," he replied softly. He held her gaze long enough for her to blush slightly and look away.

Maddie wasn't even going to try to analyze that comment right now. It was loaded with too many...ideas. His eyes had turned smoky and intense, belying the soft tone of his voice. But again, she wasn't going to think about it. Which wasn't going to prove too difficult since her stiff muscles were beginning to complain again in earnest.

She shifted slightly to try to ease the discomfort. Grimacing at the twinges of pain, she settled back in the booth. Hopefully Ash wouldn't notice.

"What's wrong?"

Darn. Luck was just not on her side this week. "Oh, my muscles are a little tight after our exercise spree today." She kept her tone light, hoping he would drop the subject.

"Judging from the look on your face, I'd say they're more than a little tight." Concern edged the deep timbre of his voice.

"It's really no big deal. I've been sore from a workout before. I think I just overdid it. I'll make sure I take a couple aspirin tonight." Thankfully the server arrived with their food. Relieved for the distraction, she quickly took a bite of her entrée, hoping Ash would drop the subject.

It was fabulous! It tasted almost erotic, it was so good. Go figure. She'd ordered a pear and blue cheese salad with champagne vinaigrette. The tangy dressing paired with the sweetness of pear and the slight bite to the blue cheese was wonderful. Amazing how such simple ingredients could look and taste so classy.

Fully engrossed in her meal, she happened to glance up and catch Ash watching her with an amused look. With a half shrug, she smiled. "What can I say? I love food, and this is one of the best meals I've ever eaten. How's yours?"

Ash didn't answer. He was too busy watching her place a bite of salad in her mouth and slowly pulling the fork out. A drop of the vinaigrette sparkled on her bottom lip. Her pink tongue easily swept it away in an unconsciously sensual movement. He looked down at his food, fighting the urge to drag her across the booth onto his lap. Leaving her alone at her door this afternoon had been one of the hardest things he'd ever done. He was paying the price for his chivalry. Not chivalry— stupidity.

It was too easy to imagine that pink tongue on his body. Maddie could kneel before him, grasp his dick in both hands and use that little tongue to her heart's content. She could swirl over the base, then slowly work her way up to the tip. He'd watch her lips slide over his shaft in the same slow motion she used with her fork. Her eyes would close and she would make the same moans of pleasure in the back of her throat. The need to see her take such delight in his taste was overpowering.

Ash was barely able to suppress his groan. This was getting out of hand. Or maybe he needed to take things into his own hands.

He'd ordered the lobster, but right now he had no idea what it tasted like. Clearing his throat, he bravely looked up at her. "Mine's great." It was all he could manage before she began her sexy movements all over again.

Her mouth opened wide enough to accommodate the salad on the end of her fork. Her lush lips closed around the tongs and drew the bite deep inside. Ash felt his erection jerk in envy. Her eyes closed while the corners of her mouth turned up in a little smile that Ash found damn sexy.

"Mmm," she sighed. "This is fantastic."

He couldn't agree more.

With strength he didn't know he possessed, he was able to look back down at his food and pretend to focus on what he was eating. Bite, chew, swallow. Bite, chew, swallow.

He finished before she did, using the time to sit back and watch her. Every now and then he'd see a flash of pain in her eyes. Hmm. She was clearly hurting more than she let on.

They both declined dessert and Ash helped her from the booth. A soft cry escaped her lips before she was able to muffle it. The guilty look she sent him had his teeth clenching. A careful, yet firm hand guided her out the door and back to her room. With every step he was aware of her fisted hands and pale face.

He should have known better than to try to cram so much physical activity into one day. Especially when they had been saving the best physical activity for tonight. But his intentions had been good. They really had.

He'd only wanted to spend the day with her and the spinning class and hike had seemed like the perfect opportunities. Ah, hell. It had all been too much. Even he was feeling a bit of a strain in his calves. Maddie's long, toned legs made it obvious she was no slouch.

Determined to salvage what he could of the evening, he led her into her room and helped her sit on the bed. Going over to the tub, he turned the water on and poured in a delicately scented bubble bath.

"Ash, what are you doing?" The perplexed look on her face was almost comical.

"I'm running a bath."

Her mouth opened and closed a few times before she finally said, "I can see that. But why?"

He kneeled in front of her and cupped her face in his hands. "Sweetheart, I know your muscles are sore and I'm really sorry I was the cause of it. What you need most right now is a hot bath and a long massage." He brushed his lips across hers, but couldn't resist the temptation to continue. Under his tender persuasion, she parted her lips. Searching the hot contours of her mouth, he was able to taste a hint of the vinaigrette. Now this was fantastic.

Cupping the back of her neck, he ravished her lips. The sweet way she yielded in his arms forced him to slow down. Soft kisses landed on the corners of her mouth. With almost painful regret, he pressed a kiss to each of her cheeks and somehow managed to pull away. How many times was that now? Ash was pretty sure he'd set the record for near misses. Resting his forehead against hers, he let out a shaky laugh. "We'd better stop if I'm supposed to remember you're hurt."

She tried to pull his mouth back to hers, with little success. "But I'm not hurt. And I've already taken two baths today."

His skeptical look was answer enough.

"Well, I'm a little sore…okay, I'm really sore. But that doesn't mean we can't make love," she hastened to assure him.

Deliberately ignoring her suggestion, he moved back to the tub and tested the water. She had no idea just how tempted he was. However, he couldn't ignore her pain. And as much as his body was begging to be inside her, that was the last thing she needed. He wanted it to be pleasurable for her. Fantastic, earth-shattering, mind-blowing pleasure. With her stiff muscles, that wouldn't happen. So instead, tonight he would pamper her…and her delectable body. While torturing his own.

Turning back to look at her, he merely asked, "Do you need help undressing?"

"Ash, really. It's not that bad."

He lifted an eyebrow. "Maddie, it's bad enough that you're biting your lip in half. Do you want me to help you undress or not?"

She hadn't even realized she'd been biting her lip. The unrelenting set of his shoulders told her if she didn't undress on her own, he'd be helping her.

Moving slowly, she worked at slipping the silk top off. Stepping out of the slacks proved to be much more challenging, but she managed with only a few whimpers. All the while he stood watching.

Embarrassed with her nudity, she moved to cover herself.

"Don't. Please." He walked over to her and lifted her chin. "Don't hide yourself from me. You're extremely sexy and I plan on seeing a lot more of your body. That's a promise. It just won't be tonight. But right now you need to get in the tub."

Warmed by the compliment, disgruntled by the way the evening was progressing, she allowed him to help her into the tub. This wasn't how the evening was supposed to go. After dinner they were supposed to come back here and make love, not have her lounge in a tub.

Alone.

It didn't matter that her muscles hurt so bad sex was probably out of the question. They had to make love. Her overactive hormones were in overdrive because of Ash and they weren't about to be denied another night.

But oh, did this hot water feel good. And the bubble bath he'd added made it smell heavenly. It probably wouldn't hurt to soak for a few minutes. Maybe then she could convince him she was feeling better.

Then again, she didn't have to soak alone, did she? "Ash? This tub is more than big enough for the both of us."

His eyes flashed at her suggestion, then shuttered. "You're too sore for me to—"

"Ash," she interrupted quietly. "I'd love for you to join me."

She could see the indecision in his gaze, but desire must have won, because he hastily shed his clothes and slid in. He sat opposite of her and took her foot in his hand. "Lay back and relax."

Happy to comply, she settled back into the bubbles and watched as he carefully began to knead her foot. His touch sent awareness dancing along her skin. As he made his way up along her calf, the firm strokes soon turned into lingering caresses.

Ash moved closer and his hands stroked their way up her thighs. "If I promise to be gentle, may I taste you?"

Her answer caught in her throat. She'd barely managed to nod before he was lifting her hips. Gently draping her legs over his shoulders, Ash bent his head to her curls. His breath puffed along her skin as he blew bubbles away.

Her eyes threatened to close, but she forced them open. She couldn't look away as Ash pressed his mouth against her. Lightly his tongue skimmed along her folds. He teased and tempted with the barest trace of a touch. Maddie couldn't suppress the trembling inside as he delved a little deeper, seeking her core. His fingers gently spread her open, exposing her.

His tongue found her center, probing inside. Her head dropped back to rest on the rim of the tub. Her hands grasped the sides almost desperately.

Ash took his time sliding his tongue in and out of her hot little pussy. Her taste was divine, as smooth as vintage cognac. Her wet heat had him craving more. When her hips began to move, he slid inside one final time. Then in a slow movement, he licked his way up to her clitoris. Maddie cried out wordlessly.

Using only his tongue, he flicked the sweet little button, wrenching more cries from her. Too intent on his goal, he took no time to find pleasure in the sounds she made. Gently he kissed along one side of her labia, then the other. He glanced over to see her white knuckles holding the sides of the tub. With more pressure, he laved her clit.

His lips closed around the sensitive nub and pulled lightly. The restless motions of her hips told him she was getting closer. Slowing down, he soothed her with long, slow laps of his tongue.

Her pleas fell on deaf ears as Ash took his sweet time tasting her. He knew how she felt. He was seconds away from his own orgasm. Her pleasure acted as the most potent aphrodisiac to his body.

Deciding to end her torment, he again took her clit into his mouth. Sucking harder this time, he felt more than heard her crest rising. Ash flicked his tongue firmly against her. Alternating between laving and sucking her clit, he soon brought her over the edge with a shattering sob.

For many minutes neither said a word. The subtle sound of bubbles popping along the water was the only noise to be heard.

Her head lolled against the edge of the tub, making Ash smile. He had to get out of the bath before he really did forget she was hurt. She made a small sound of protest when he hopped out and toweled off.

"Maddie, do you have any lotion?"

She watched him move around, obviously searching. "Mmm…there should be some in my bag."

"Perfect," she thought she heard him mutter, as he disappeared around the corner. Too wrung out to go after him, she closed her eyes and let her mind wander. Ash was amazing. His mouth was amazing, his touch was amazing…

What seemed like scarcely a minute later she heard, "Sweetheart, it's time to get out." The voice was quiet, deep. She ignored it.

"Maddie, the water is getting cold." Sleepily she blinked her eyes open. The deep voice belonged to Ash. Then she remembered where she was. In a tub of quickly cooling water with very few bubbles left.

He handed her a towel and she sleepily stood to dry herself. Some of the stiffness was definitely gone, but her movements were slow and cautious. Still painful.

Ash was watching carefully and she knew she wouldn't be able to fool him into thinking she felt much better. She didn't know if she had enough energy to even make the effort.

He didn't give her a chance to speak, but motioned her to the bed. "Okay, why don't you lay down and I'll give you a massage."

She collapsed onto her stomach, more than willing to let him. A few seconds later she felt his hands sweeping her hair off her shoulders.

"Don't want to get lotion in your hair."

"Mmm," she mumbled drowsily.

He warmed the lotion in his hands and started with her shoulders. Maddie practically purred with delight. The lightly scented lotion, the right amount of pressure, and Ash's hands weren't too bad a way to spend the evening. If they couldn't have sex, this had to be the next best thing. It was still a long way off from what she'd originally envisioned, but it would have to suffice.

He methodically worked his way down her back. When he got to her backside, she couldn't help but tense slightly.

"Relax," he commanded, in a voice gone husky.

Once his hands started working on the sore muscles, she was able to. He hit a few tender spots and she couldn't quite stifle her groans of half pain, half pleasure. She only hoped the massage therapist she had an appointment with tomorrow was half as good as Ash.

Continuing down her legs, he worked tirelessly until her limbs felt like Jell-O. All the while she moaned and groaned like a woman being pleasured. Hey, it wasn't technically passion, but he was touching her in what she thought was the second most pleasurable way a woman could be touched.

During his ministrations, Ash desperately tried to think about anything and everything but the creamy, soft skin beneath his fingertips. As well as the erotic little sounds coming from between her sweet lips. He was so damn hard right now, he knew no control panel in the world could help him. Her taste was still on his lips. He didn't think he'd ever forget it. However, considering her condition, it would probably be best if he tried.

Ash could sense her total relaxation, so he took his time massaging his way back up her body. The movements of his hands became much more sensual, but no less adept. He caressed the long length of her thighs, vividly imaging how they would feel spread beneath him. Wrapped around him.

Grasping the smooth roundness of her cheeks, he marveled at their firmness. Damn, this woman was built to pleasure a man's senses as well as his body.

Smoothing his hands over her back one last time, he gently rolled her over. Her groans had stopped some time ago, but he'd been too aroused to notice. When he saw her face, he wasn't surprised to find her asleep. Disappointed, but not surprised. And like a man in love, he took it all in stride.

Love.

He tested the word on his lips. It felt right. Maddie felt right, both beneath his hands and in his heart. This amazing emotion had snuck up on him quickly, but he was more than happy to accept it.

He carefully tucked the sheets around her. In her sleep, she scrunched up her face and snuggled deeper into the bed. Smiling at the picture she made, he reclined beside her and rested on one elbow. For over an hour he simply lay there, stroking her hair, holding her close. Marveling that he'd been lucky enough to find the woman of his dreams.

He was completely in love with this woman. And he only had three days left to show her just how right they were together. With a sigh at the daunting task he had before him, he stood to leave. Tomorrow was going to be a busy day.

Chapter Ten

ɞ

Maddie stretched luxuriously and rolled over. That had been one of the best nights of sleep she'd had in a long time. According to the alarm clock it was only 7:30. She lay there for a few moments, trying to recall what her schedule was for the day.

Stretching again, her hand found a piece of paper on the pillow next to her. Memories of the night before assailed her. Oh no. Ash had been here last night. And she'd all but passed out when he had given her that heavenly massage. She hadn't even said thank you before he left. Or given him a goodnight kiss.

Feeling guilty and embarrassed, she looked at the note. The words were written in short, precise strokes.

You were sleeping so peacefully, I didn't want to disturb you. Hope you're feeling better this morning. I'm playing a round of golf today and won't be done until early afternoon. I'd like to try dinner again tonight.

Love, Ash

Her heart tripped, stumbled and continued its descent.

He'd taken care of her last night.

It was difficult for her to remember the last time someone had been there to take care of her. And done it in such a selfless and tender way. The tug to her heartstrings this time was much more insistent. Ash had worked his way under her skin and was getting much too close to the vicinity of her heart.

Ruthlessly pushing aside the frightening thought, she re-read the note. It was surprising he wanted to try dinner again. Their two disastrous and ultimately frustrating dates certainly weren't the kind that would encourage a guy to come back for more. Especially when there were so many other guests here who would love to keep him happy. So why did he? Maybe he figured the third time would be the charm. She was praying it was. If one more night with Ash was wasted, she would seriously consider becoming a nun. Well, maybe not a nun, but she'd at least swear off dating for another few years.

Placing the note on the nightstand, she figured it was time to see if the massage had helped any. Cautiously she sat up and swung one leg, then the other off the bed. There was still discomfort, but it had been reduced to a dull throb rather than the sharp pain of yesterday. Heaving a sigh of relief, she stood up slowly.

This morning she had a body wrap and massage scheduled, which should take care of any lingering stiffness. It would also help to keep her occupied until she could see Ash. And she wanted to see him. To thank him for the massage, of course, but the sooner she saw him, the better. She planned on thanking him in a very satisfying way.

The big box of condoms shouldn't go to waste. Neither should the rest of this vacation. *Kris went to great lengths to con me into it*, Maddie thought wryly.

Right now she needed her daily intake of coffee. Showering quickly, she hurried down to the dining room. Half hoping Ash would be there, she was disappointed when she didn't see him.

The only other patrons in the room were two middle-aged couples and the same group of women who'd been on the hike yesterday.

Oh well, she thought. She'd be seeing him in a couple hours, which would be soon enough. It wasn't as if she would spend the morning pining away for him. That would make it seem…as if she had feelings for him. No, there were plenty of things to keep her occupied.

Watching the two couples swap kisses and grope each other wasn't on the agenda.

In record time, she finished her food. It was becoming easier to stomach the phallic-shaped fruit. And the *Kama Sutra* helpful hints were definitely more entertaining than the weather forecast and latest investment news she'd find in her daily newspaper.

Once back in her room, she decided to read. If a book couldn't keep her mind occupied, nothing would.

As it was, thoughts of Ash intruded on every other page. She barely managed to finish a chapter before it was time for her appointment. It was discomfiting that for once, something, or rather *someone*, had interrupted her reading. Usually once she was immersed in a book, nothing shy of an earthquake could rouse her. Then again, Ash's effect on her could be compared to an earthquake. A life-altering earthquake.

Dropping the book on the nightstand, she stood and stretched cautiously. Time for her body wrap and massage. A few hours of pure indulgence would definitely help to take her mind off this situation that was rapidly getting out of hand.

When she reached the spa, the doors once again opened to reveal the perfectly blonde Bree. Her eyes lit with recognition and a genuine smile as she spotted Maddie. "Hello, Ms. Summers. Ready for that body wrap and massage?"

Maddie brought her hand to her sore thigh in an unconscious gesture. "Definitely. I took a spinning class yesterday and topped it off with a hike."

"With Shannon?" At Maddie's nod of confirmation, Bree winced in sympathy. "Ouch. I've taken a class by Shannon before. Only once and it was more than enough. She can be brutal. But at least you were able to get out of bed. We've had a few guests who've taken her class before and were so sore they had a massage therapist come to their rooms because they couldn't move."

Laughing, Maddie had a good idea most of the guests probably used sore muscles as an excuse to get a therapist in their room, but not for a massage. "You're telling me. I soaked in three hot baths yesterday and even that didn't help."

"Well, you're scheduled for the massage first, so you will hopefully be feeling better in an hour. You're right back this way." She led Maddie past the hairstyling room, and down a short hallway. At the end of the hall to the left was a small room with an open door. Bree beckoned her inside. "If you would like to remove your clothes and get settled on the table, Jared will be with you in a few moments."

The door closed softly behind her and Maddie turned and inhaled the relaxing aromas infusing the room. Flickering candles filled the space with the delicate scents of lavender and vanilla. Hopefully they would help to relax her, she thought, with a dubious stare at the massage table in the middle of the room.

She'd never had an actual massage before and wasn't quite sure how she felt about stripping down to nothing. Especially when the person who'd be putting his hands on her was a stranger named Jared. Who also offered oral stimulation.

Wait a minute. She was supposed to be a new and improved woman. One with plenty of courage to deal with the opposite sex. Besides, the oral stimulation was an option she'd decided against.

Shaking off the momentary doubt, she bravely stripped down and lay on the table before she could change her mind. Settling the sheet around her, she tried to focus on anything and everything but the fact she was now naked. And about to be manhandled by a professional oral stimulator.

With a snort, she realized how ridiculous she was acting. Jacques had recommended Jared for this massage, so Maddie hoped things would be okay. Besides, maybe he was—

Her brain did a mental jaw drop. Gorgeous!

The door had opened to reveal a tall, bronze Adonis. Was everyone in this place beautiful?

In a low, almost melodious voice, he introduced himself. "Hello, Ms. Summers. I'm Jared. Bree told me you experienced one of Shannon's spinning classes yesterday, so this is probably just what you need right about now."

Surprising herself, she was somehow able to say, "F-from what she told me, I'm not as bad off as some guests have been."

A small smile moved his sculpted lips. Lips that most of his female clients probably had serious fantasies about. Oral stimulation took on a whole new meaning when you saw those lips. "No, you're not. You must have caught her on a good day. Before we get started, are there any areas that are especially bothering you?"

The question immediately revved her libido into high gear. As a matter of fact...

Taking a moment to remember to breathe, she finally said, "Just my legs and feet. They bore the brunt of it." The rest would have to wait until tonight.

"Very good. We'll see if we can't get you feeling better." He turned on a small CD player in the corner of the room and seconds later she heard the sound of soft guitar strings. Noting she was on her back, he asked, "Why don't we have you lay on your stomach and place your head right here to start with." He gestured to the small headrest, which happened to be directly in front of — and level with — his crotch.

Well now, this could be interesting.

She rolled over and hesitantly put her face on the headrest, pleasantly surprised to find it wasn't as uncomfortable as it looked. Despite the close proximity to Jared's...

If she didn't have sex tonight, she'd go insane. Or explode.

Conscious thought flew out the window as he began to knead her back and shoulders.

Oh, that was soooo good...

Silently retracting her early thoughts, she was positive it wasn't his lips that had female clients coming back for more. Today wasn't going to be the day she found out about the other. If anyone was going to have their lips on her, it would be Ash.

Last night he'd more than proven how adept he was in that department.

Jared continued to massage her, allowing her mind to roam about Ash and his lips. Lips that would stimulate nerve endings that hadn't seen the broad side of a testosterone-packed male in too many months.

With a mental groan at her one-track mind, she tried to concentrate on the massage. It didn't take long for it to demand her complete attention. Jared had just reached her hamstrings and the massage had reached the fine line between pleasure and pain.

Her teeth clenched as the line was crossed. It took all her effort to keep from crying out. "You might experience some tenderness in these areas tomorrow."

It couldn't be any worse than what she was experiencing now. After swallowing a groan, she replied, "That's okay. It won't be anything like what I would have felt if I hadn't come in."

They lapsed into silence as he carefully worked his way down her legs. By the time he reached her feet, she was as limp as a rag doll. Maybe regular massages were another thing she'd have to look into when she got home.

All too soon, the massage was over and Jared was saying, "All done. Hopefully that will give you some relief and you'll be moving a bit easier." Pointing to a white spa robe, he continued, "When you're ready, go ahead and put on the robe. You'll find Mandy in the room directly across the hall, where you'll have your body wrap. She's all ready for you over there. "All she could manage was a drowsy nod in his direction. When he stepped out of the room, she sat up on her elbows. That had felt wonderful. Her body was relaxed and rejuvenated. More than ready for an evening with Ash.

Smiling with satisfaction, she stood up and shrugged into the robe. Securing the tie, she walked across the hall, where she was met by a short, dark-haired woman wearing a beaming smile. And the typical spa uniform of little else. Streaks of silver were shot through her hair, pronouncing her to be older than at first glance.

"Ms. Summers? I see Jared got you nice and relaxed for this. We'll get you wrapped up and you can lie back for about an hour."

"Sounds great."

Maddie had mistakenly assumed they only offered the chocolate or whipped cream body wraps. So she was surprised when Mandy asked her, "What body wrap are we doing today? You have your choice of the chocolate or whipped cream. We also have the more traditional seaweed wrap, mud wrap or the herbal wrap."

Maddie's confusion must have shown, because Mandy smiled. "The chocolate or whipped cream wraps can be applied by one of our attendants. Bryan and Jack were both Chippendale dancers at one time, and Daniel used to model underwear. And they're all very good at what they do." She punctuated the comment with a wink. "I do the other wraps. You'll see the benefits to your skin with one of those, but most of our guests aren't here for that."

Maddie shook her head. "No, I think I'll stick with one of the traditional wraps." The last thing she needed was to be around any more…stimulation. She asked, "Which one would you recommend?"

After surveying her with a critical eye, Mandy replied, "I would go with the mud wrap. Your skin will feel amazing afterward."

Figuring Mandy had to know what she was talking about, Maddie agreed.

After being painted from neck to toe with a surprisingly pleasant-smelling mud concoction, she was wrapped in heated strips of cloth and left to relax for an hour. Her eyes slowly drifted shut, lulled by the warmth of her cocoon, and she slept soundly until Mandy came back.

Once Mandy had the mud cleaned off, she held out a robe. As Maddie drowsily placed her arms in the sleeves, Mandy pointed to an overstuffed chair in the corner of the room. "You can go ahead and relax over there if you like. I'll get you something to drink. Would you like some herbal tea?"

"Sure. That sounds great." Maddie was more than happy to sit and relax. Between the wrap and the massage, she felt completely wrung out in a delicious, languorous way.

Mandy came back with a steaming mug of tea and made sure she was settled back comfortably in the chair. "Let me know when you finish that cup and I'll get you another. It's really important to replenish your body's fluids after the wrap and massage."

Maddie dutifully took a sip of tea. It wasn't her drink of choice, but she figured she might as well take in the whole spa experience. Considering how many times they'd offered her this herbal tea, it seemed the right thing to do. She only hoped it wasn't spiked with anything…strange.

Thirty minutes later she was back in her own clothes and feeling much, much better. Leaving a generous tip for both Jared and Mandy, she left the spa. She debated heading back to her room to finish her nap, but her growling stomach refused to be ignored. Nourishment was her biggest priority at the moment, but only because Ash was nowhere to be found.

Hoping she'd be able to eat alone today, she headed for the casual restaurant. A furtive glance around the seating area assured her no unwanted single men were in sight. Unfortunately, one wanted man in particular wasn't in sight either. But it was okay. She was a big girl who was more than able to eat lunch on her own. Feigning an indifference she didn't quite feel, she ordered lunch and sat back to wonder, not for the first time, what Ash was up to.

* * * * *

Irritated and physically frustrated beyond endurance, Ash stomped into his room. That had been the worst golf game he'd ever played. Not only that, it had by far been the most humiliating. Thankfully none of his golf buddies had been there to witness it. Their good-natured ribbing would have turned into astonishment coupled with uproarious laughter.

Never in his life had he missed hitting the ball, let alone three times in a row. And especially not while two little old ladies looked on. Their helpful though very much unwanted advice had embarrassed him. Though not as much as their lack of clothing and continuous catcalls. When he'd finally managed to hit the damn ball, they'd praised him loudly, amid invitations to let them "have a try at swinging his club and whacking his balls".

It had only gotten worse.

He cringed just thinking about the poor guy who'd barely moved out of the way in time to miss the flying golf club at one of the holes. Ash hadn't meant to let go. He really hadn't. But his grip had gone slack when he'd thought about Maddie's nipples hardening from his caress. Then there were the two simple putts on holes five and seven that he should have had no problem with. Instead of making the shots, he'd been too busy envisioning Maddie's pale, firm buttocks beneath his hands. Her long legs wrapped around his waist. Her full lips on his…

Needless to say, his score hadn't been worth keeping track of.

Growling his frustration, he sat on the bed and cradled his head between his hands. This was getting out of hand. Though he had truly enjoyed getting to know her body last night, it hadn't been enough. Not tasting her, nor massaging her.

More than anything, he'd wanted to stay with her. Hold her all night long next to him. Wake with her. Make love to her. And when they'd exhausted themselves, he had wanted to tell her how he felt. Shamelessly spill his guts to her. Offer his heart on a silver platter, whatever it took as long as she knew. And then make love to her all over again.

At the moment, however, his emotions were on the back burner. The desire he felt for her had increased into a raging inferno and his body was on fire. He had to have her.

Now.

Because despite the chilling nightmare his twisted mind had conjured, he would bet his last dime that no control-top brief could contain the erection of painful proportions he was currently sporting. Which was yet another reason why his golf game had been so off. A guy has to be balanced, and he'd been so off balance since meeting Maddie he was surprised he could function. That and it was probably a health concern to have such a large quantity of your blood pooled in one place for so long. Not only was he off balance, but his blood circulation was in jeopardy.

Enough fantasizing.

Surging to his feet, he left his room in search of the hazel-eyed vixen who was slowly driving him crazy. Driving his body, mind, heart *and* soul completely crazy.

His knock on her door was answered with silence. Working unsuccessfully to unclench his teeth, he tried to take a few deep breaths to calm himself. She had said she was going to be at the spa, so most likely she was still there. His mind was able to assimilate that possibility, but his body didn't care.

Today, however, someone finally took pity on him.

"Ash! I'm glad I found you. I was just wondering if you were done with your game."

Maddie.

It was a strange combination of relief and wild lust that raced through him at the sound of her voice. He spun around toward her. "Game? Oh, my golf game. That was a lost cause from the beginning. Can we go inside?" His words were harsher than he'd intended, a direct result of the sharp edge of desire riding him.

Surprise mingled with confusion on her face. "Um, sure. Is everything okay?"

"No."

As soon as she had the door unlocked, he rushed inside, pulling her along with him. She must have realized what the sound of the slamming door signified because her eyes widened.

She took a wary step back as he took a step closer. He had no idea the gleam in his eyes went beyond predatory. Soon she was backed up against the wall, his body crowding hers. He watched her nervously lick her lips. "Ash, what are you doing?"

His smile was feral as the hunger inside him demanded appeasement. In a voice barely above a growl, he explained, "First I'm going to kiss you until we both can't breathe. Then I'm going to take your clothes off, place you on the bed, and make love to you. Hard."

A breathy "Oh" was all she managed before his lips claimed hers. The kiss seared him. He had thought he might have to coax a response out of her, but she surprised him. Her arms wrapped tightly around his neck and her hot mouth was open and eager beneath his. All he could think was that he was finally going to make her his.

Chapter Eleven

෨

Maddie was nearly overwhelmed by the barely leashed passion she'd seen in his eyes moments before he'd crushed her to him. But her body's response quickly squelched any doubts. This was what she'd been waiting for. Her skin felt hypersensitive and she wanted, no, *needed* his hands on her.

Pressing herself closer, she left him with no doubt as to her wishes. Her hands moved continuously over his body as the kiss went on and on. With her fingers, she memorized the hard planes of his chest, the ripples of his abdomen, the sexy indentations near his hip. The hot length of him pressed insistently against her soft belly and she groaned.

Grasping his sexy, firm butt, she pulled herself closer, instinctively cradling her hips in his own. She needed him inside.

He broke their embrace long enough to hastily rid them of their clothes. She saw his nostrils flare slightly and his eyes flash with approval at her nude body. This time she felt no shame, no embarrassment. Only an exhilarating certainty that Ash truly found her sexy and beautiful. The rosy flush that tinged her body was fueled by the hungry way he looked at her, nearly devouring her with his eyes.

In the same low, sexy growl he'd used earlier, he rasped, "Sweetheart, I promise that next time I'll take it slow and make sure we have time to savor each other, but right now I just have to have you."

Her only response was to open her mouth for another kiss. She found herself quickly deposited on the bed, their mouths still fused together with a desperate need. They'd been denied too long to make this first time last.

With undisguised longing, she watched him rip open the foil packet and quickly cover his straining erection. The man was absolutely magnificent. Though he gave her only a brief moment to look her fill, what she did see caused her to inhale sharply.

Mistaking her response for fear, Ash froze. She watched the muscles in his body tighten as he fought for control. "What? What's wrong?" When she didn't immediately answer, he followed the line of her gaze. Again, he misunderstood her reaction. "Maddie, I promise I won't hurt you. I know I'm rushing things here, but I'll make sure you're ready for me before I—" Her finger against his lips stopped the rest of his strained dialogue.

Willing him to meet her gaze, she let him see that it was wonder and anticipation in her eyes. And rather than puff up in pure male arrogance, Maddie was amazed to see a faint blush stain his cheeks. It was quickly followed by a small smile.

"Oh," was all he said.

"I was thinking more along the lines of 'wow'. And if you don't hurry, I will be in pain." She barely recognized the throaty voice as her own.

Still he held back. "How are you feeling today?"

Feeling? He wanted to know how she was feeling as she was sprawled naked on the bed, her body flushed with unfulfilled desire? Shouldn't it be obvious? Then it hit her. He was asking about her sore muscles.

Time slowed as she felt her heart stumble, trip, then fall completely and hopelessly for him. Gulp.

She opened her mouth a few times before she was actually able to speak. "Um, thanks to you, I'm feeling good." When he flashed his heart-stopping smile, she flashed one of her own, allowing her mind to fill with him and only him as she whispered, "And I know if you come a little closer you can make me feel a whole lot better."

Needing no other invitation, he moved between her legs. He groaned his approval when he found her already wet for him. As slowly as he could manage, he entered her. Inch by hard, satisfying inch.

"God...Maddie...you're so hot and tight." With a low, hoarse cry, his final shred of control snapped. Her gasp of surprise echoed his groan of pleasure. For a minute neither of them moved, but simply savored the feel of one another.

Ash no longer felt empty. With her, inside her, he now felt...complete.

As he had known it would, her body fit perfectly with his. Her full breasts and rosy nipples begged for a taste. Her long legs were wrapped tightly around him. Her hands were curled against his chest. But it was her eyes that held him. Desire had deepened the green flecks. She was staring at him with a need that mirrored his.

Perfect.

He was given no time to lose himself in her gaze as her curvy hips bucked beneath him, demanding. More than willing to oblige, he began sliding in and out. Her inner muscles held him tight, causing him to grit his teeth at the pure pleasure. Purposely keeping the tempo slow when she would have tried to rush him. Wanting the sensations to never end.

"Easy, sweetheart. We'll get there together." Even if it killed him.

However, she was more determined than he imagined. Maddie pulled his head down for a deep kiss. Their lips pressed together and her tongue slid inside his mouth. They broke apart for air and she took the opportunity to press soft, teasing kisses along his jaw. When she found the sensitive spot on his throat, he instinctively began to move faster, harder.

Softly moaning her approval, she continued her pleasurable torture along his throat, up to his ear, her soft lips nibbling on his skin. "Mmm," she purred into his ear. "You taste wonderful, as I knew you would." Her hands moved around him to grasp his buttocks firmly, then glided up his back in soothing strokes.

Rearing back onto his knees, he grasped her legs and placed them over his shoulders, lifting her hips slightly and allowing himself deeper penetration. Ash watched her mouth part slightly as he thrust slow and deep for a few minutes.

Just as her breath began to quicken, he stopped and drew her legs from his shoulders. Ash lifted her hips and placed them on his thighs. Placing her legs once again on his shoulders, he grasped her waist and pulled her slowly onto his shaft.

Her eyes closed and her head fell to one side as he thrust deep inside her heat. Unconsciously, she squeezed her thighs together, creating more friction every time Ash slid inside.

God almighty, she was going to be the death of him. She'd claimed she had very little experience with this, but her actions were those of a born seductress. She met him stroke for stroke. He prayed she was close, otherwise he was really going to embarrass himself.

At that moment, he felt her muscles begin to clench around him as she dug her nails into the sheets. A look of rapture came over her face as her orgasm crested, pulsing around his shaft. When she cried out his name, he instantly found his own release, his hoarse cry echoing in the room.

More than a little stunned at the intensity, he all but collapsed on top of her. He knew he was probably crushing her with his weight, but he couldn't move. His heart was pounding so hard, he knew she had to feel it.

When she squirmed beneath him, it took supreme effort to move, but somehow he managed it.

A few minutes later, when he was fairly sure his legs would hold him, Ash got up to dispose of the condom. He returned to the bed and lay down beside her, pulling her close. Staring up at the ceiling, he marveled at the sense of peace and contentment seeping through him. This was right.

Together, they were right.

Maddie was still too exhausted to move. She had seriously underestimated him. She had known sex with Ash was going to be incredible, but that…that had been beyond anything she could have imagined. It had been hot, fast, and at the same time, oh-so sweet.

Long minutes passed before either found the strength or breathe to speak. Ash looked down at her. "What are you thinking?"

She smiled, staring at the ceiling as he had done minutes before, and replied, "Your name doesn't quite suit you."

His brow furrowed. "It doesn't?"

"Ash is the result of a fire that is long dead, but what I just experienced was," she gestured weakly with one hand, "explosive. I'm still burning with the aftershocks."

She turned in time to see his smug grin.

Honey, he thought to himself, *the flame between us will burn for a long, long time. I don't plan on ever letting it go out.* But instead of voicing his opinion, he simply pulled her closer.

Making love to her had been beyond even his vivid imagination. The look on her face when they'd both found their release would be forever engraved in his mind. He planned on doing everything and anything he could to make sure he saw that look often. As often as possible, in fact — starting now.

Maddie had other ideas. A glance at the clock told her it was shortly after two in the afternoon. Perfect. The yoga class they'd agreed to do didn't start until three, which meant they had just enough time to shower and change. There was no way she was letting him get out of it, amazing sex or not. She thought it was only fitting payment for the topless spinning class.

Reluctantly sliding from his embrace, she sauntered over to the bathroom. She threw him a quick glance over her shoulder and said, "Our class starts at three. We have just enough time to shower and get over there."

"Class?" He raised a brow at her.

"Sure. Don't you remember? We have the yoga class today." Before he could argue, she slipped into the shower.

As she expected, there was a muffled oath and he soon joined her in the oversized shower. "Do you mean to tell me that you actually expect me to go to a yoga class after that?" He spit out the word "yoga" as if it were something distasteful.

Humming under her breath, she lathered her hair with shampoo and gave him a sudsy smile. "You bet."

His capable hands grabbed the soap and began washing her in long, slow caresses. His husky whisper reached her ears. "You mean you'd rather be twisting yourself into a pretzel instead of staying here? Because I'm sure we could find some positions in bed that would be much more…satisfying."

He'd lathered his fingers and was busy soaping her breasts. Leaning back against the tiled wall, she closed her eyes. Mmm. His hands were tempting her all over again. Ash made lazy circles, rubbing his thumbs over the stiff peaks of her nipples. Moving lower, he lightly traced down her stomach, teasing the skin around her belly button. His fingers dipped lower still, and all too quickly she was ready for him.

Hadn't they been discussing something? Oh, right. The class. Mustering all her strength against the demanding pull of desire, Maddie grabbed the soap from him and began to return the favor. Swirling her fingers in the soapy mat of hair on his chest, she gifted him with a smile full of promise. "No. I'd rather be in the yoga class getting nice and limber so we can come back here later."

Ignoring her words, Ash deftly pulled the soap away and held her hands. "As much as I'm enjoying this, we didn't grab protection. And I don't want to risk falling on my ass as I walk across the floor dripping wet to get some."

"Well, I would." The words were out before she had time to think them through. But the knowing grin he gave her made her slip worth it. Heaving an exaggerated sigh, she conceded, "But I suppose you're right. Especially since we don't have a lot of time to get to our class."

He grimaced at the reminder. "You really want to see me suffer for those sore muscles, don't you?"

"Not at all," she laughed. "What I want is to see you trying to twist into a pretzel."

A serious note entered his gaze. "Are you sure you're feeling better?"

"Didn't I just prove it?" She had to laugh as his eyes flickered at the reminder. "I'm sure. I had a massage right before I came back here." She gave him a playful shove. "And the yoga will help too. Trust me, you're not going to talk me out of that class."

His answer was to pin her up against the shower wall and nearly crumble her resolve yet again with a soul-shattering kiss. Her body instantly responded, nipples hardening to rosy peaks, mouth opening to accept his tongue's caress, arms entwining around his neck. One of his hands was busy teasing her nipple while the other grasped her hip. Had the shower suddenly become hotter?

More than ready to forget the yoga class, she was surprised when he pulled away. "Mmm. As much as *I* would like to finish *that*, you want to get to class. We would hate to be late for it." Ash then had the nerve to throw her a wicked grin, give her a light swat on the rear and step out of the shower as if completely unaffected.

Warm water cascaded around her, feeling almost cold against the heat he had created. The man knew how to kiss. Unfortunately for her, he also seemed to know how those kisses affected her. Blowing out a shaky breath, she managed to rinse the last of the shampoo out of her hair. A few minutes alone under the water allowed her time to compose her shaky nerves. Somewhat.

When she finally stepped out, he was standing in front of her with a towel. "I've brought a peace offering." Did he mean the towel? Or himself, standing there with a poor excuse for a towel wrapped low around his hips? A towel which did nothing to hide just how affected he really was.

Hiding her small smile of perverse victory, she accepted the towel with as much grace as the situation allowed. Feeling a little wicked, she proceeded to give him a taste of his own medicine as she dried herself off. Slowly, sensually, she rubbed the towel against her wet skin. At least she hoped it looked sexy. Rubbing along her arms, down her breasts, taking great care to catch every last drop of water. A moment later, she turned in time to catch his hungry expression. And, she noted with satisfaction, his towel was starting to slip under the...pressure.

"A peace offering for what?" she asked, with her most innocent expression. Spreading her legs, she dried first one and then the other, making sure Ash saw the towel glide up and down.

His raised his gaze to her face. "Peace offering? Oh, because—" Her intentions must have shown on her face because he shook his head ruefully. "You little tease. Okay, we're even now." He heaved an exaggerated sigh and looked at her with a pitiful, woebegone expression. "So what should I wear for this class?"

She eyed his towel thoughtfully. "I'd say under present circumstances, that towel won't work. A pair of shorts and a tank top or T-shirt should be fine. Whatever's comfortable for you."

He threatened to let the towel drop and smiled suggestively. "Getting rid of this would be more comfortable for me. The only thing that would make it better is you doing the same."

Her first urge was to agree with all possible haste. Oh boy was she tempted. But her head was still looking to sort through the mess her heart was in. Yoga always helped her to regain her focus. Plus, after his little tease in the shower, he deserved to have to sit through an hour of yoga. "Hold that thought until after the class."

The dejected slump of his shoulders was almost comical. "Rejected for a yoga class. How low can a guy get? Okay, I'll just go grab my clothes I guess. I'll be right back," he grumbled.

When he threw her one last hopeful glance over his shoulder, she resolutely ignored him. Before he closed the door, she heard him mutter, "It damn well better be the naked yoga class."

Stifling a giggle, Maddie pulled a pair of yoga capris out of her suitcase. She'd made sure it was a regular yoga class, so Ash was out of luck. Until they got back to the room, that is. Humming under her breath as she dressed, she wondered if he'd try to find any other excuses to keep them here. Part of her hoped he would.

She didn't have to wait long for Ash to return, no excuses on his lips. He was still looking a little perturbed and very sexy. Maddie couldn't resist placing a brief kiss on his lips. "You weren't kidding when you said you have the stamina of a stallion."

The twinkle returned to his eyes as he laughed with her. "Sweetheart, you bring out a side of me I've never seen in myself. Can you blame me for not being able to get enough of you?"

He didn't appear to require an answer to that question. Which was good, because Maddie had no idea what to say. In fact, it was a question she could ask herself about *him*. And she wasn't quite ready to analyze the answer.

To hide her confusion she ignored the comment and said, "According to the class schedule, it looks like we're in the room next to where we took the spinning class."

Tucking her hand in his, he said in an agonized tone, "Might as well get this over with."

"Come on, you big baby. It won't be that bad. You'll see."

* * * * *

Maddie's reassurances didn't help. It was that bad. And that good. Ash was still staggered by his feelings for this woman. He'd had no idea that making love to her would feel so right. As if he'd finally found where he belonged. And who he belonged with. All he wanted right now was to be back in bed with her. Exploring her, exploring these emotions and savoring the feeling of just being with her.

Instead he found himself in a yoga class sitting on what Maddie had called a sticky mat. Who would want to sit on something called a sticky mat? He sure didn't. The thin layer of rubbery, sticky foam between his rear and the floor seemed to be a wasted effort anyway. But the smile on Maddie's face had him keeping his complaints to himself. She obviously wanted to take this class. Truth be told, he wanted to take it just so he could be near her. There was also the added benefit of seeing her in the snug, formfitting yoga outfit.

The room quickly filled and Ash found himself next to a balding, middle-aged man in spandex shorts that were a few sizes too small. Spandex was supposed to be fitted, but the way it fit this guy was…well, it just didn't look healthy. He hastily turned his head to where Maddie sat at his left. The view was much, much better.

Glancing around, he was somewhat surprised to see a total of four men in the class, himself included, as well as seven women. It was a relief to see he wasn't the only man in here. Judging by the pained expression on the younger guy in front, he wanted to be there about as much as Ash did.

The two men exchanged a look of pure male disgust at the whole affair. Then the man looked at the woman next to him and lifted a shoulder as if to say, *the things we do for love*.

Smiling to himself, Ash could only agree. He had a feeling that before this was through, Maddie would have him wrapped around her little finger. Lucky him.

A door off to the side of the room opened and the instructor walked in. Both he and Maddie heaved silent sighs of relief when they saw it wasn't Shannon. Instead of the perky brunette, they had a tall, willowy blonde in a royal blue sleeveless catsuit, who looked to be anywhere between the age of thirty-five and fifty.

In a soft voice, she introduced herself. "Hello everyone. My name is Shelia. I'm glad to see we have a nice turnout for today's yoga class. To give you a little background, I've been teaching yoga for almost fifteen years. I teach three different classes. This class is designed for beginners, but I modify it for those at the intermediate level as well. Today we'll be working on a variety of asana. Now, does anyone have any questions before we begin?"

As someone took the opportunity to ask a question, Ash leaned over to Maddie and whispered, "Assa what?"

"Asana. The yoga poses."

He nodded in understanding, when he really didn't understand at all. The clock on the wall told him only two minutes of the one-hour class had passed. This was going to be a long afternoon.

All too soon, the class began. The first thing they did was lie in what Shelia called Corpse Posture.

"The Corpse Posture will help you to relax your body and mind so that when we continue with each asana you will be able to focus better and get the most from this class."

Ash thought the name was a little morbid for someone trying to achieve total relaxation while still alive. Lying there on the floor sprawled out like a dead guy, he listened to the soothing voice of the instructor as she moved from person to person, helping them to correct their posture. When she got to him, he received a beaming smile. "Very good," Shelia praised.

Nearly snorting with disgust, he wondered how many people could screw this up. How hard was it to sprawl out on the floor? Wisely not voicing his musings, he allowed himself to relax back into the pose. He could admit it was pretty comfortable. Here he thought he was going to have to try and contort his body into all sorts of weird positions.

A short while later, Shelia began to instruct them into other poses. Downward Facing Dog almost proved to be his undoing. As Shelia came around to show him how to adjust his legs, he began thinking he might need to take up a stretching routine when he got home.

While everyone else in the room seemed to be perfectly aligned, Ash was having trouble just keep his butt up in the air while his hands and feet were still on the floor. No matter what Shelia said, there was no way his heels were ever going to be flat on the floor.

The only gratification he got out of the pose was when he looked over and saw Maddie's sweet little rear high in the air. He had about two seconds to admire it before he toppled over.

"Oh my gosh! Ash, are you okay?"

Doing his best to appear unperturbed, Ash brushed off Maddie's concern. In a low voice intended for her ears only, he said, "You are going to owe me for this." This class would unman him if he didn't start paying more attention to keeping his balance and less attention to Maddie's...assets.

She flashed him a sweet and deceptively innocent smile before scrambling back to her mat.

The next pose he felt even remotely comfortable with was the Staff Posture. After watching Maddie stretch and twist her lithe limbs, he felt the name was apt. He'd been doing his best to hide his staff for the past fifteen minutes. Yes, she would definitely pay for this class later. Like a trooper, he willingly sat with his legs stretched out in front of him and his back straight. There, that wasn't too bad.

"Okay, now make sure you lift your chest. There, that's great. Focus on keeping your diaphragm relaxed," Shelia advised the class.

Ash was having no problem with tension in his diaphragm, but other parts of him were not so cooperative.

Throughout the class, Shelia described what each pose was good for. Ash wondered if she had anything to help ease an erection. There seemed to be yoga postures for every other ailment, why not that? And while he'd heard that yoga would help you relax and become more limber, he found himself more wound up and tighter than ever. Of course, that could be because he was watching Maddie.

A few minutes later, he was vowing that this was the first, last and only yoga class he would ever take. When Shelia moved them into the next pose, Ash knew he was in for it. At her instruction, the class knelt on the floor and slowly bent their backs, tipping their heads backward and holding their heels with their hands.

"This is the Camel Posture. It's a wonderful pose for relieving stiffness in the back, shoulders and ankles."

The Camel Posture? Ash assumed they were supposed to resemble a camel's hump. He was barely able to tip his head back, and there was no way he would be able to hold his heels and resemble anything remotely like a camel. A curious glance at the guy next to him was a big mistake. The guy was obviously a yoga regular because he was able to do the pose and earn a smile from Shelia. In this position, his spandex shorts were showing everyone a lot more than they wanted to see. Well, a lot more than Ash wanted to see. The guy was taking the camel hump a little too far with what his spandex was revealing.

Averting his gaze, he looked over to Maddie. This time her pert breasts were being shown off to their full advantage. Now this was more like it. This was a Camel Posture he could handle. Or at least he wished he could handle.

Unfortunately there were still fifteen minutes left in the class. Thankfully Shelia let him off the hook when she announced the last fifteen minutes would be for the intermediate level class members. With barely disguised hunger, he watched as Maddie shifted herself into a perfect headstand, followed by what Shelia called an Upward Facing Bow Posture. To Ash it looked like an inverted version of the doggie pose. Either way, he could only admire the way her back arched into a graceful curve as she lifted her torso toward the ceiling while leaving her hands and feet on the ground.

His erection was definitely not in manageable proportions at the moment and this certainly wasn't helping. He could only be thankful he wasn't in spandex like the camel guy. In a desperate attempt to regain a semblance of control, Ash looked away and his gaze happened to rest upon a woman who was also in the Upward Facing Bow Posture.

Yikes.

His first instinct was to immediately close his eyes, but some perverse side of him, a side that was seemingly drawn toward the stranger things in life, forced him to look on in morbid fascination.

Instead of wearing tight spandex shorts like the camel man, this woman was wearing a top that would have been much more appropriate on a…well, he wasn't sure if it would have been appropriate on anyone. It was cut low in the front and would normally have showed off a decent—make that indecent—amount of cleavage, had it been on anyone else. Like someone who wasn't pushing sixty. However, in this particular position, her breasts were doing their best to do their own pose. Which involved touching her nose. And it wasn't because they were well-endowed. It was more because they were very, very tired and wanted nothing more than to let gravity do its thing and let them rest.

On the ground.

Ash knew how the combination of time and gravity could work against a person, man or woman, but this was just…well, it wasn't pretty.

Yikes, he thought again.

Boy, if that picture hadn't worked better than a cold shower, he didn't know what would. And as much as he wanted to be thankful for the short reprieve, he didn't know how long it would be before he'd forget that particular image. It was almost worse than being propositioned by the grannies earlier.

He was wondering if he'd sustained permanent psychological damage when Maddie touched his arm. "Ash? Ready to go?"

They were done? Hallelujah. His day had just brightened considerably. "Sweetheart, I can't begin to tell you just how ready." With all possible haste, he steered her away from the yoga room and all of its weird positions and protrusions and back toward their rooms.

The more he thought about it, the more he was beginning to become seriously concerned about any permanent damage. What if he and Maddie were about to make love, and thoughts of…*that* kept him from getting it up? What if his dick hung limp for the rest of his life just like that woman's breasts?

Performance anxiety, the deep, gut-wrenching fear only a male can fully comprehend, took root and forced him to increase his pace until they were practically running for their rooms.

Laughing, she tugged on his arm. "Hey, slow down. You're supposed to feel nice and relaxed after that. Not ready to go out and run a marathon."

The look he gave her was full of pure heat, he hoped, as he replied slowly, "I just saw you move your body into all sorts of different positions. Now where exactly do you think I'm running to?" *Her body, Maddie's body*, his mind chanted. *Maddie's young, luscious body, with everything in the right place. Long legs, full hips and full, pert, perky breasts.*

A delicate blush stained her cheeks as comprehension dawned.

"Sweetheart, I really need to do a better job if you've forgotten everything so soon," he teased. *And I need to simply do the job so I can forget everything that I just saw as soon as possible*, he thought anxiously.

She met his gaze. "Believe me, I didn't forget."

"Good," came his satisfied answer. According to the stirring in his shorts, he hadn't forgotten either. His shriveled ego lurched with hope at the telltale movement. They reached her room, but he led her past it and into his.

Once inside, he saw the question in her eyes. Rather than answer right away, he pulled the band out of her hair, watching intently as the glossy strands cascaded down to rest on the tops of her shoulders. He lifted a silky tendril between his fingers and murmured in a distracted tone, "This time I want to see you in *my* bed. With your hair spread out over *my* pillow."

"Mmm. I like the sound of that." Right before he could claim her lips, she pulled away and moved toward the door. "Just let me grab a few things from my room."

He snaked an arm around her waist as she reached for the doorknob. "Don't bother getting any clothes. You won't need them. In fact, the only thing I was hoping you'd need at the moment was me." The teasing tone he used took most of the arrogance out of the statement.

The searing kiss he'd planned to place on her lips missed by a few inches and landed on her cheek when she moved her head. She waited until she held his frustrated gaze before asking bluntly, "Do you have any condoms?"

"Yeah. I think I have…uh…somewhere…" he trailed off. Well, damn. He had only one condom with him and he knew that wasn't going to cut it tonight. In his haste to find her this afternoon, he'd forgotten to stop at the gift shop.

With great reluctance, he released her. "You'd better go grab some. But don't take too long. Please." God forbid she took longer than a few minutes. Long enough that he had time to remember what he'd seen only moments before. Right now, certain parts of him were having no trouble defying gravity. But he'd seen how easily gravity could take over.

He almost began to shudder with dread, when he saw her lips curve into the siren's smile he loved so much. "Don't worry. I'll be back before you know it."

He watched until she had disappeared into her room. Closing his eyes, he clung to the vision of her smile. His own lips curved into a very satisfied grin. Oh, yeah. His sexy Maddie could produce the desired results with only a smile. To hell with gravity.

Chapter Twelve

࿇

Maddie walked into her own room in time to hear the phone ring. Who in the world would be calling? Ash had seemed extremely reluctant to let her leave, but he wouldn't be calling her in her own room when she'd promised to be right back, would he?

She lifted the receiver to her ear. "Hello?"

"Maddie? Is that you?"

Oh, she knew that voice. "Kris?"

"Who else? I'm sorry to bother you but I've been dying up here. How is everything? Are you having fun? Have you met any hunks or are there just old people like you thought? How's the spa?"

Laughing, Maddie tried to stem the barrage of questions. "Slow down, slow down. Everything is fine. The spa treatments have been heavenly. As much as I hate to admit it, I owe you big-time for this trip. I didn't realize how much I needed it until I got here."

"Of course you did." Maddie could just imagine Kris waving away her words. "That was a given. But you didn't answer me. Are there any other singles there? Particularly, gorgeous single males?"

"There's a little bit of everything here," Maddie replied in a dry tone.

The snort on the other end of the line told her she wouldn't get away with that kind of vague answer. "Come on, spill. Have you met any available guys or not?"

Twirling the phone cord around her fingers, Maddie debated. "Well, let's see. There was the shuttle bus driver, who stripped down to a thong when I got here. There's the guy who goes around having sex in various public places, but he's usually taken when I see him. Oh, and there was the guy who gave me a massage today. He specializes in oral stimulation."

Kris whooped so loudly, Maddie had to pull the phone away from her ear. "I knew it! Aren't you glad I packed that little gift for you? Oh, I knew those would come in handy."

Maddie wasn't about to give Kris anything, so she responded with, "Mmm-hmm."

"Well, come on! I want details here. What are their names? What do they look like? And more importantly, how is the sex?"

Kris never had been one for subtlety or beating around the bush. Maddie hesitated a second too long before answering.

"Maddie? You still there?"

"Yeah, I'm still here. No, I didn't have sex with any of them."

"What!? Are you crazy? How could you pass up sex with a guy who specializes in *oral stimulation*!?"

"You just asked about sex, Kris. Not anything else." Maddie couldn't help the impish smile that crossed her face.

Wild laughter erupted in her ear. When it finally subsided, Kris immediately resumed her questioning. "Have you had one of the Toe Fetish Pedicures? I don't know about you, but just the thought of some hunky guy sucking on my toes then painting them makes me hot."

Dropping her head into her hands, Maddie could only groan. Enough was enough. She wanted an explanation. "Kris, you sent me to an *erotic resort*!"

"I know! Isn't it great? That place has gotten some great reviews. Have you had a chance to try the *Kama Sutra* class yet? Or what about the—"

Sparing the phone a withering glare, Maddie knew she wasn't about to get an apology. And she really hadn't expected one. Instead she cut Kris off. "Oh, gee. Look at the time. I'm late for my next appointment. Gotta go!" Then she hung up with a gratifying click.

No way was she going to give Kris the satisfaction of knowing whether or not she was participating in any of the classes. Or having amazing sex.

Speaking of amazing sex, she needed to get back to her "appointment". Grabbing her lip gloss, she slicked her lips with the peach-flavored concoction before turning around—and running right into Ash.

"Easy there. Sorry about that, I thought you heard me come in." He steadied her.

"No, I was on the phone with a friend of mine. She called to check up on me and make sure I was surviving my *Kama Sutra* lessons."

He raised a brow at that. "Now there's an idea. It has definite possibilities."

"I think there's a better possibility of me going back to your room with you."

His sexy grin nearly stopped her heart. "Sweetheart, I can't argue with that idea."

Maddie looked at the gorgeous man in front of her and felt a pang of regret. Here was the most wonderful guy she'd ever met and it was only meant to last for a few days. It was too late for her to keep her heart, but she wasn't so foolish to let this time slip through her fingers.

She would simply enjoy the next couple days with him to the fullest. If she had any say in it, she would more than make sure he enjoyed himself just as much. When Saturday came she wouldn't regret her time with him. Neither would she forget it.

Needing a change in scenery as well as a distraction, Maddie grabbed the box of condoms. "Okay, I got what I came for. How about we rendezvous back at your room?" The invitation was punctuated with what she hoped was a seductive smile.

Ash's gray eyes probed hers, probably seeing more than she wanted him to. But he allowed her to escape. Flashing her that sexy half grin, he slid a finger down her bare arm, causing her to shiver. "You haven't come yet, sweetheart, but I promise you will soon."

Her body was instantly aflame. She wanted it soon. Needed it now. Before he could see the steam rolling off her in waves, she hurried out the door, knowing he was right behind her.

The grin slowly faded from his face as Ash followed Maddie back to his room at a slower pace. He'd seen the emotion in her eyes. He could recognize it, because he felt it too. But she wasn't ready to admit to it. For some reason, she wasn't yet ready to face those feelings. Which proved he still had a fair share of convincing to do.

Little more than two days remained. For a man who was able to move business deals along in record time, this should be no problem. But where matters of the heart were concerned, there were never any guarantees. Fortunately, he planned on there being only one outcome. Him. Maddie. Forever.

He stood at the threshold of his room, staring at Maddie, who was already inside. Waiting. For a moment, he allowed himself to consider the situation. She waited for his body, while he waited for her heart. The smile on his face should have been a warning to her. Soon she would know she could have his body and with it his heart. And soon, she would give him hers.

The door closed softly behind him.

This woman, who at times was both innocent and sassy, had wanted a week of hot sex. She had chosen him as much as he had chosen her. And hadn't she said he created a fire within her? *Well sweetheart*, he thought with wicked intent, *get ready to play with fire. And I'll teach you exactly how to fan those flames so they never go out.*

* * * * *

Maddie inhaled sharply at the look on Ash's face. What was that saying? Something about if looks could kill? Judging by his expression, he wanted her to burn. And the hot flame of desire that shot through let her know she was more than willing to do just that.

Her pulse drummed rapidly as she waited. Yet he stood there, watching. It was almost as if he was waiting, too. She knew he was as aroused as she. The evidence was clearly outlined in his shorts, not to mention the hungry gaze he'd locked on her. Yet he made no move to come closer.

What was he waiting for? A sign? She was pretty sure the box of condoms she still held in her hand made her wishes fairly apparent. Or maybe he was waiting for her to make a move. Hmm. The thought was definitely tempting. Oh, who was she kidding? The thought of her being the aggressor this time turned her on.

Not taking her eyes off him, she placed the box on the nightstand next to the bed, where it would be within reach.

Never in her life had she tried to be a temptress. But for Ash, she would. The way he was staring gave her the extra boost of confidence she needed.

Hips swaying seductively, she walked toward him. When she was mere inches away, she stopped. Her hands came to rest lightly on his chest, swirling in lazy circles over his taut muscles. She watched him from beneath lowered lashes, almost missing the slight flaring of his nostrils.

Perfect.

A small smile curved her lips while her hands continued their languid exploration. "Ash, I'm really glad you came to that class with me."

"No problem." His voice was low and only a tad bit husky.

She looked up at him, letting him see the amusement in her eyes. "Oh, I know you hated every second of it." One hand had skimmed beneath the soft T-shirt he was wearing.

His eyes darkened as she moved her fingers through the light mat of curls on his chest, and then slowly followed the silken trail to where it disappeared into his waistband. This time his response was slower in coming. "Ah...well...I didn't hate *every* second."

"Really?" She tugged the shirt over his head. She pulled him back toward the bed and maneuvered him around so the backs of his legs pressed against it. With a light push from her, he sat down. "You didn't seem too happy to be there, and you were more than happy to leave."

"I think it's safe to say yoga is not my thing."

Smoothing her hands over his shoulders, she leaned closer. "That's too bad. There are so many...benefits to yoga." When he still made no move to touch her, she straddled his thighs. Maddie knew he was allowing her to take control and she wouldn't let either of them regret it.

A sharp intake of breath was the only answer she received.

Maddie pressed hot kisses along his jaw, down his neck, the length of one shoulder, then the other.

This time his voice was hoarse with desire. "What...what benefits would those be?"

Her tongue had found the sensitive spot near his ear and her teeth gently grazed his skin before she answered. "It's amazing how limber a person becomes after practicing yoga for a while."

She had moved onto the other ear, drawing a shudder from him when she blew lightly on the sensitized skin. "Li-limber?"

"Mmm-hmm. Your body is able to move into so many graceful positions."

His hands tangled in her hair as he grasped her head and pulled her close for a kiss. Their mouths fused together, hungrily searching. For a moment, she let him take control of the kiss. Needed to feel his hunger. Seconds before she became completely overwhelmed, she pulled back. "Ah, ah, ah. You said next time *I* would be able to explore. Well, it's next time, and I want to explore."

His eyes flashed with something she couldn't quite name. Satisfaction? Arousal? Triumph? It was gone too quickly for her to tell. His hands dropped to his sides and he leaned back on his elbows in acceptance. Such a deceptive pose.

Standing up before she lost her nerve, she yanked on the edge of his shorts. "These definitely have to go."

The sexy quirk to his lips was back as he obligingly lifted his hips for her. That little half grin seemed to dare her to go further. So he wanted to play, did he? He must not have believed her when she told him she was going to explore. If nothing else, she planned on doing a very thorough exploration.

She pulled his shorts and underwear off in one tug and watched his erection spring free. Wow, he was beautiful. Long, straight and hard, his penis was extremely well-proportioned. The heat consuming her had risen a few degrees. She planned on saving the best part for last, otherwise it would be over a lot sooner than she had anticipated.

Moving her gaze leisurely up his body, she took note of each dark hair, every hard ridge. He interrupted her perusal. "I think it's only fair your clothes come off too."

"Hmm," was all she said, as she lowered her mouth to one of his small, dark nipples. She grazed the sensitive flesh with her teeth, soothing with her tongue when he groaned. He fell back completely onto the mattress and closed his eyes as she continued her sensual assault on the other one. Never had she wanted to taste a man as she did Ash. Never had she craved hot, male flesh like she did his.

For tonight, he was hers. She wasn't going to waste a second of it.

Maddie sat up and pulled off her yoga top. She'd worn no bra underneath, so he was instantly rewarded with the sight of her rose-tipped breasts. Without thought, one hand came up to cup her breast, but she stopped him. "Sorry, but you can't touch until I'm done exploring."

The challenge in her eyes was clear. She didn't think he could do it. Gritting his teeth, Ash drew his hands up over his head, where he clenched them tightly together. He might not be able to do it, but she knew he'd hold out as long as possible.

Maddie stood to pull off her pants, revealing a black lace thong. It hadn't been the most comfortable thing to wear during a yoga class, but judging from the look on Ash's face it had been well worth it. His eyes had widened and the muscles in his arms were corded tight, as if fighting to keep his hands to himself. In this instant, she felt as if she were the most desirable woman in the world. Only Ash had ever made her feel that way.

In unhurried, deliberate movements, she once more straddled him. Her hot center pressed intimately against his well-defined stomach. Yes, tonight was going to last as long as she could make it.

While he watched her from beneath lowered lashes, she leaned over him. She lightly nibbled at the corners of his mouth. Her breasts brushed against the dusting of hair on his chest, bringing her nipples to hard peaks. Moaning softly, she allowed herself to sample his lips. They opened with little persuasion, both hard and yielding at the same time. Her tongue danced along his. His arms came up to encircle her and bring her closer. When he tried to take control, she pulled back.

Carefully, she moved from his embrace. Shimmying down his body, she nearly crested when she rubbed against the hard length of him. His quick intake of breath assured her he was close as well. Resisting the urge to repeat the movement, she rested herself on his thighs.

Maddie bent forward to place a kiss below his left hip. Deft fingers traced the contours of his abdomen. Goose bumps followed in their wake. Moving to the right hip, she ran her tongue along the sensitive indentation. His involuntary shiver only served to heighten her desire. She noticed his hands were clenched in the sheets, and had to smile.

Up along his stomach she went, taking time to delight in the salty tang of his skin. He muttered under his breath as she took light nips here and there. Hiding her smile at his discomfort, she appeased with small strokes of her tongue.

When she was satisfied with her exploration of his navel, she gave him no time to recover as she filled her hands with his pulsing erection. A small bead of moisture gleamed on the engorged tip. Smiling with anticipation, she looked up to see him watching her intently. She held his gaze as she slowly, slowly closed her mouth around him. For a moment she simply reveled in the taste. Hot. Salty. Wonderful.

Ash nearly shot off the bed at the feel of her hot mouth. "Maddie!" The rough cry was torn from his lips.

One small hand cupped his balls, while the other stroked his shaft, following the motion of her mouth. This was torture. The most incredible, erotic torture he'd ever endured. He didn't even realize when his hands tangled in her hair.

Her lips moved along the length of him, tasting him everywhere. Her tongue swirled around his engorged head. Wave of sensation after sensation crashed into him. Head thrown back, eyes closed, he allowed himself to embrace the pleasure she so willingly gave.

Over and over, she stroked him. Then she stopped and pressed her mouth along the underside of his dick. Her tongue came out to lick along the length of him. Ash shuddered when she took the tip of him into her mouth and gently sucked.

Resuming the long strokes with her hands, Maddie took him deeper into her mouth. His hips lifted involuntarily, forcing his dick further down her throat. She hummed softly, sending a jolt throughout his whole body.

When he neared the brink, he gently tugged on her hair. "Maddie, sweetheart…you…you have to stop."

Maddie lifted her head. Her tongue—that wonderful, amazing, perfect tongue—swept across her lips. "I had no idea you'd taste so good."

Those simple words nearly made him explode. Hissing through his teeth, he fought desperately to remain in control. He closed his eyes and focused on deep breaths. Inhale, exhale. Inhale, exhale.

A small noise distracted him enough to make him open his eyes. Maddie had torn open a foil packet and was moving toward him. This woman was definitely going to be the death of him.

He watched her in part fascination, part raging, out of control lust as she placed the condom on the tip of his shaft. She rolled it down in excruciatingly slow movements. Words were well beyond his capability. He watched as she quickly removed her thong before positioning herself above him.

Her very talented hands guided him toward the place he most wanted to be. Again, with excruciatingly slow movements, she slid down on him, enveloping him in her hot, tight sheath. It was obvious that giving him pleasure had given her pleasure as well. She was so wet, he slid in with little effort.

Desperately, he grabbed her hips when she would have moved. "Please…if you have any mercy, don't move."

She must have known how close he was, because she held very still. Five seconds passed. Ten seconds…

Exhaling a loud breath, he brought his hands up to her breasts. He lightly flicked each nipple. She moaned faintly, her inner muscles clenching him tighter.

Urging her closer, he drew one pert nipple into his mouth as she began to rock above him. Suckling gently, then harder matching the motion of their hips, he wrung another moan out of her, louder this time. Drawing a hand from her breast, he grasped her hip and drove himself deeper, lifting them off the mattress.

She began to ride him harder and his hand dropped to where their bodies joined. His thumb found her clit amid her wet curls. Ash stroked the sweet little nub, wanting to hear her cry out. He smiled against her breast when she obliged him.

"Ash! Oh, god...Ash!"

He felt her begin to tighten around him. His teeth nipped at the sensitive bud in his mouth as he pushed her over the edge. She was still crying out his name when he came.

Ash was fairly sure he'd died and gone to heaven. He knew his heart had stopped at that final moment when they had simultaneously reached their climax. And when it had resumed beating, he would swear the cadence beat to the time of her name.

She was sprawled atop him. If not for her unsteady breathing and the pounding of her heart against his chest, he might have thought she'd fallen asleep.

Somewhat bemused, he found his hand trembling as he stroked her hair. Rather than frowning at the less-than-masculine display, he felt a sappy smile widen across his face. Oh yeah, this love stuff was pretty damn great.

"Maddie?"

She didn't move.

He lowered his voice to a whisper. "Sweetheart, are you asleep?"

She still didn't move, but said in a husky whisper muffled against his chest, "No. I'm just trying to remember who I am and where I am. You said my name is Maddie?"

He chuckled while she slid off him. Flopping down beside him, she threw her arm across her face, all the while keeping her eyes closed. Which about summed up how he felt too.

Ash disposed of the condom, then sat next to her. Because he couldn't seem to stop touching her, he threaded his fingers through hers. The arm that was across her face lifted a fraction and her eyes fluttered open. She didn't realize her heart was in her eyes when she looked at him. But Ash noticed.

It was all he could do to keep himself from going down on one knee and declaring his love. Old-fashioned and foolish, yes, but he was beyond the point of caring. Unfortunately, she wasn't ready. But the love was there, which was enough for him.

For now.

Her voice broke through the silence. "I'm not even going to try to explain what just happened." Sweet lips that had long since lost their peach gloss — on him — turned up in a smile. The temptation was more than he could resist. Bending forward, he took a quick taste.

Desire slammed through him at the gentle contact, but he was able to keep the kiss sweet and soft. Sitting back, he took a fortifying breath. She needed to recuperate for a while. A short while. He looked around for a distraction. Something, *anything* to get his mind off her.

No, she was a permanent fixture in his thoughts, but he did need to refocus on something other than her body for a moment.

"So…" he struggled to find a safe topic.

She must have seen his discomfort and took pity on him. After covering herself with a sheet, she sat up. "I'm starving. If you're going to keep this up, we should probably warn the chefs here that I'll need sustenance every couple of hours."

A teasing glint sparkled in his gaze as he replied, "I hate to break it to you, but you're the one keeping it up. I'm completely blameless."

"Ha, ha. Aren't you the comedian?" She threw a pillow at him.

Laughing, he caught it and set it aside. "Do you want to order room service?"

Maddie looked down at the sheet wrapped around her. "That's probably a good idea."

* * * * *

Thirty minutes later they were busy eating the tray of food Ash had ordered. When Maddie had seen the food, she'd merely raised an eyebrow in question. It was a feast fit for a porn king.

His sheepish shrug had been endearing, but the wicked smile he flashed ruined the whole effect. "You said you'd need sustenance."

"Yeah, but not for a whole horny army."

He shrugged again, unrepentant. With a shake of her head, she started on the bowl of fresh fruit. She was starting to grow fond of the phallic shapes.

When they'd both eaten their fill, they snuggled on the bed. His arms came around her and pulled her close. Maddie closed her eyes, savoring the feeling of security. She should have been surprised how easy it was to simply be with him. After the mind-blowing sex they'd shared, this should have been awkward. But it wasn't. Instead it felt comfortable.

It felt right.

Before her mind veered off into dangerous territory yet again, she brought her fingers up to play with the hairs on his chest. She didn't like to think of herself as shallow, but one thing she'd never been able to stomach was a hairy man. When a man had so much hair it grew thicker on his back than it did on her head, that was where she drew the line. Thankfully, Ash wasn't anywhere near that line.

She wrapped her finger around a small tuft of hair and tugged playfully.

"Ouch." He grabbed her hand before she could do it again. He had been dozing lightly, but now aimed a warning glance her way.

She pasted an innocent smile on her face and slid her fingers free. Her fingers walked their way down his chest, down his stomach, pausing to lightly trace the small trail of hair that led to his shaft. Which was growing by the second.

Once again, he grabbed her hand. "Did the food help to revive you?" His tone was hopeful.

"Definitely. You?"

With one quick motion, she found herself on her back staring up at his glittering eyes. "Definitely." His mouth lowered to hers.

The kiss had all of the heat and passion as before, but his lips were also tender. One hand cupped the back of her neck as he tasted her. Moaning against his mouth, she brought her hands up to stroke his back, delighting when the muscles rippled from her touch.

As she had done, he pressed kisses against her jaw, her neck. Shivering at the contact, she tipped her head back to allow him better access. He was in no hurry as he slowly and deliberately feasted on the creamy skin at the base of her throat. Her hands moved lower to grasp his taut buttocks and pull him closer, craving the intimate contact.

His head came up as he stared down at her. "You got to explore last time. Now it's my turn."

His deep, husky voice melted her insides as liquid heat pooled in her stomach and lower. The implication in his tone assured her that he would give as well as he got. And considering what she'd given to him… Another moan escaped as her muscles tightened in anticipation.

His lips returned to her throat before leisurely moving across her collarbone and down, finally coming to a stop at the top of the valley of breasts. Her breath caught in her throat as he took one hardened peak into his mouth. When his tongue flicked the rosy tip once, twice, she arched into his mouth. Minutes passed as he indulged his cravings. He hadn't even touched her anywhere else and she was already nearing her climax.

"Ash, I need…" she trailed off as his hand skimmed down her stomach.

It took a second for her to realize he'd stopped at the top of her curls. With a whimper of frustration, she lifted her hips, silently urging him to touch her.

"What, Maddie? Tell me. Tell me what you need."

The words were ripped from her throat as she arched beneath him. "Touch me…please just touch me."

"Gladly, sweetheart." And he did. He slid one long finger inside her while his thumb began to caress her clitoris. The pressure started to build inside once more. Another finger joined the first in her moist heat as his mouth met hers. Short, precise strokes brought her closer. His tongue slid in and out of her mouth in time with his fingers.

Maddie was disappointed when he moved his lips to her neck. But only for a second.

Ash spread tender kisses along her neck, pausing to sample the tender skin. His mouth moved much lower, to her hip, mimicking her earlier actions. She sucked in a quick breath when he slid his tongue down her hip and along her thigh. He lingered alongside her inner thigh, inhaling the spicy, sweet scent of her arousal.

"Ash, I don't think—"

"Perfect," he interrupted her plea. "Don't think at all, sweetheart. Just enjoy for me."

One hand spread her delicate folds, displaying the perfect feast before him. Maddie clutched the sheets, as he had before. Features taut with desire, he lowered his mouth to her curls.

She cried out when his tongue found her clit. He held her hips still as he tongued her. Ash couldn't resist burying his tongue deep inside. He could taste her desire, feel the heat of it surround him. It was more delicious then he remembered. *She* was more delicious.

His fingers took over, finding the perfect tempo for her restless hips. Taking her clit into his mouth, he pulled lightly on the most exquisite part of her. Her moans grew louder as he sucked harder, knowing she was close to reaching her peak. How quickly he'd learned exactly what sent her over that cliff.

With the expertise of a skilled lover, he brought her to a shattering orgasm. Ash couldn't help but savor her cries of pleasure from his intimate kiss.

Maddie's body was still thrumming with passion when he rolled on a condom and slid into her. Aftershocks caused her inner muscles to clench around him, forcing a low, sexy growl from his throat. Long legs immediately wrapped around his waist as he began to thrust. Gripping her hips, he lifted her slightly, allowing him to glide deeper.

She took his face in her hands. Bringing their lips together, she closed her eyes at the taste. She was on his lips. Never had anything tasted so perfect, or so right.

His thrusts became faster as her hips urged him on. Nails scored his back as the sensual friction increased. She couldn't get enough of this man.

Maddie felt the muscles in his back tighten as he neared his release. His eyes were closed, his head thrown back. The look on his face was one of pure ecstasy as he came in a blinding rush.

He dropped his head onto her shoulder as he tried to slow his breathing. She wrapped her arms around him, holding him close as the sensations and emotions overwhelmed her senses. Briefly she wondered if it would always be like this. Just as quickly, she dashed the thought from her mind. She only had two more days with this amazing man. She'd save her heartbreak for when she got home.

He rolled to his side as he pulled out of her, rising to dispose of the condom before lying back down and pulling her close. The tender kiss he placed on her forehead nearly brought tears to her eyes. Ducking her head against his shoulder, she prayed he wouldn't see. Minutes passed and not a word was spoken. Eventually, his deep, even breathing let her know he had succumbed to his exhaustion. The steady rhythm of his chest rising and falling lulled her into slumber as well. And neither loosened their hold on the other.

* * * * *

The next time Maddie opened her eyes, night had fallen. An alarm clock on the nightstand said it was nine o'clock in the evening. She'd never fallen asleep so early in the afternoon. Then again, she'd never had such great sex before. A quick glance at Ash made her aware he too was awake, and watching her with a small smile.

"Hey," she said softly, suddenly overcome with self-conscious shyness.

"Hey yourself." He idly twirled a strand of her hair between his fingers, though his gaze never left her face.

Uncomfortable under the scrutiny, she dropped her gaze to his chest. Her emotions were still too raw to risk looking into his soulful eyes. She had a feeling he saw much more than she intended.

Her stomach chose that exact moment to rumble loudly. It wasn't the most sophisticated way to be rescued, but it worked. Maddie smiled sheepishly. "Needless to say, I'm starving."

"What a coincidence. I am too." He leaned over for a kiss, making it very clear what he was hungry for.

"No, no," she pushed him away, laughing. "I'm hungry for *food*. You know, that stuff that your body needs to survive?"

Disappointment flashed quickly over his face, then was gone. "I suppose you're about due for your sustenance, aren't you? But how do you know my body doesn't need yours to survive?" She made no response.

Heaving an exaggerated sigh, he helped her out of bed and handed her a hunter green, terrycloth robe to step into. The sleeves had to be rolled a few times before she could see her hands, but she loved it. The oversized robe was ultra-soft and smelled like Ash — earthy, male and very sexy.

She was busy smelling the collar when he cleared his throat. "Um, is there something wrong with the robe?"

She felt a hot blush warm her cheeks. "Nope. It's just fine."

"Are you sure? Because I could have sworn you were sniffing it."

"Well, ah…I was." He raised a brow, waiting for her to elaborate. "It, um…" She blew out a breath. "It smells like you."

A curious light entered his eyes. "So, is that a good thing or a bad thing?"

"Oh, it's a good thing. Definitely a good thing."

Instead of his signature half smile, this time his face split into a wide grin. Not fair. He was even more gorgeous when he did that. Charcoal gray sweats that had been carelessly pulled on rode low on his lean hips. Teasing her because she knew what lay beneath the waistband. Yum. Unable to stop staring, she felt her pulse jump when he moved closer. But all he did was press a warm kiss to her forehead. "Maddie, you really are something else."

It wasn't exactly the most romantic thing a man could say after the greatest sex of her life, but she flushed with pleasure nonetheless. Coming from Ash, it meant quite a bit. Giving her no time to think about it, he drew her toward the table and chairs. Checking the various platters they'd tucked away in the fridge, he studied what was left of their early dinner. "Okay, let's see what we have left to eat here."

Under one of the trays, he found two turkey wraps with salads to feast on. He handed her one of the plates, and also grabbed two bottles of sparkling water to complete the meal.

Maddie dug in with her usual gusto. She was so hungry, it took a few minutes to realize that Ash might be a little shocked at the way she was eating. Warm, gray eyes met hers as she looked up to gauge his reaction. It was amusement rather than disgust that colored his tone when he said, "If you showed even a fraction of that hunger for me, I think I'd be a dead man."

"But wouldn't you die happy?" she asked with an exaggerated wink, her shyness from moments before pushed aside.

"I'll drink to that." He saluted her with his water bottle and took a long drink.

Twenty minutes later, she was feeling much better. At least her hunger for food had been sated. Ash had finished his food a few minutes before her and was busy picking through the fruit tray.

She had just popped a red grape into her mouth when he asked, "So what's your favorite type of book?"

Chewing slowly, she thought about it. "It really depends on the mood I'm in, but I tend to go back to mysteries and romance novels."

He lifted an eyebrow. "Romance, huh? Now why doesn't that surprise me? Let me guess, your favorite stories involve Vikings named Leif who wield a huge sword. Or a gun-slinging cowboy named Clint who keeps his gun well oiled and knows how to make your day."

Maddie gave an inelegant snort of disdain. "You've got to be kidding me."

But Ash was on a roll. "No, it's probably about some Scottish guy named Ian who's hung like a bull and likes to show women what's under his kilt."

She quickly covered his mouth before he could continue. "You know, if I didn't know any better, I would be really worried about how well you warmed to that subject."

The teasing glint in his eyes swiftly changed to affronted male pride as he glared. But he didn't say a word. Probably because she was still covering his mouth.

"Now, are you done?"

Her only answer was a lowering of his brows. She was really having trouble holding her serious expression in place. "If you really want to know, my favorite story is about a guy named Ash who has the stamina of a stallion."

She was laughing too hard to stop him from grabbing her and throwing her on the bed.

"Laugh it up, sweetheart. Just remember, revenge is sweet." That said, he began tickling her. How he knew that she was extremely ticklish, she had no idea, but she was gasping for breath by the time he finally allowed her to escape.

"I give! I give! Uncle! Mercy!" she cried, in between spurts of laughter.

He removed his fingers from her ribs and sat up against the headboard, pulling her along so that she lay with her head on his chest. "If you're ready to have a serious conversation, we can try that again."

"If I'm ready…" she sputtered. She tried to lift her head, but he kept it firmly against his chest. "I'm not the one who started spouting off about well-hung Vikings and horny cowboys."

"You didn't have to. You're the one who reads about them."

He was baiting her and she knew it, but it was still difficult not to react. So she settled for ignoring him. "I also like to read mysteries and the occasional biography."

"Hmm," was all he said. His hands were busy playing with strands of her hair. Almost absently he murmured, "You know, my parents would love you. Especially my mom. She's always admired a woman with a little spunk."

Maddie stiffened in his arms. His parents? Was he thinking he wanted to introduce her to his family? She worked hard to ignore how her heart jumped at his words. She ruthlessly squashed the small, giddy bubble of hope that threatened to form. It didn't matter if he thought his parents would love her. Well, it shouldn't matter. But it did.

So she did the only thing she could think of to distract herself. She cupped one hand around his penis and lifted her head so her lips could find his. He immediately hardened and their lips met, muting their hungry groans of desire.

Mere seconds later, the conversation was all but forgotten as they once more climbed the peak to ecstasy. Some time later, they fell asleep in one another's arms.

Chapter Thirteen

෨

On Friday morning, Ash made the transition from deep sleep to drowsy wakefulness slowly. His eyes remained closed as he allowed his other senses to wake. Because he knew he probably had a foul case of morning breath, he decided to forgo his sense of taste. Inhaling deeply, his nose picked up the scent of freshly brewed coffee. His ears heard a slight rustling noise, as if someone were moving around. He swept his hand over the sheet next to him.

No Maddie.

Opening his eyes, he saw her just as she sat down at the small table. If he could wake up to this every morning, every day would be the best of his life.

Ash drank in the sight of her like a man dying of thirst. Her hair was in tousled disarray around her head. On anyone else it would have looked messy. Maddie simply looked sexy. She had thrown on one of his T-shirts and the hem rode high on her thigh. High enough that when she had sat down he'd glimpsed a tantalizing view of the curve of her sweet ass.

As his gaze traveled leisurely upward, he spotted a small love bite at the delectable curve where her shoulder met her neck. The telling mark sent an odd thrill through him. Call him chauvinistic, but knowing that she'd be walking around with his mark on her skin made him feel pretty damn good. It wasn't a permanent mark, but it would have to do for now.

After a mental pat on the back, he finally looked at her face. His feeling of triumph withered at the sight he encountered.

Maddie looked miserable.

Of course, they hadn't gotten much sleep the past two nights, but they'd had enough she shouldn't look as exhausted as she did. It wasn't even the circles under her eyes that bothered him. It was the sad, haunted look within them. The dejected slump of her shoulders. The way she drank her coffee without seeming to taste it. This was definitely not the same woman who'd taken such pleasure in her cup of coffee a couple days ago.

What was wrong?

His gut clenched at the thought that he hadn't given her pleasure the way she had him. Then he remembered the way she'd all but come apart in his arms.

Each and every time they'd made love.

A frown creased his brow. No one was that good of an actress. Hell, the past two days he'd had the most amazing sex of his life. They'd talked, cuddled and had more amazing sex. He could probably use another few hours of sleep himself, but all in all, he was feeling better than he could ever remember feeling. In fact, he was pretty sure he'd be wearing a goofy grin on his face all day that would shout, "I'm in love!"

So why was she looking as if her best friend had died?

She didn't even notice when he sat up and climbed out of bed. He walked toward her and said quietly, "Good morning, sweetheart." And because he couldn't help himself, he kissed her softly on the lips.

When he pulled back, she'd pasted a patently false smile on her lips. "Morning. I hope I didn't wake you up. I tried to be as quiet as I could when I got the coffee started."

A yawn escaped before he could stop it. Stretching to relieve some stiffness, he raised his arms above his head. "No, you didn't wake me up." He absently rubbed the back of his neck before he noticed her eyes had dropped to his morning erection. Under her intense scrutiny, it twitched and lengthened.

With a blush staining her cheeks, she wrenched her gaze away, staring at something to the right of him.

He wanted to laugh. Comfortable in his nudity, he surmised she was not. She'd been as wild and uninhibited as he had, but this morning she was shy and nervous. He loved what a contradiction she was.

"As you can see, I missed you when I woke up. I wanted to wake you up slowly."

Amused, he watched her lick her lips nervously as she looked everywhere but at him. "Oh, well...I, um, was having trouble sleeping and thought some coffee would help."

"Has it?" He stretched again, watching her through lowered lids. Oh, yeah. He had her attention now.

She blinked rapidly. "Has it what?"

"Has the coffee helped?"

"Um..." she stared blankly at the mug in her hands. "A little, I guess."

He brought her attention back to him as he rubbed his stomach in an absent manner. "Well, I don't know about you, but I could use a shower." It was flattering to watch her eyes widen and darken with desire.

Without waiting for a response, he turned and walked into the bathroom. Before he stepped through the door, he looked over his shoulder and caught her staring at his ass. He felt those caveman tendencies welling up inside as he fought the need to howl and beat at his chest.

Thank God she still wanted him. But what could have put that look in her eyes? As he turned on the water and adjusted the spray, he thought about anything that might have happened to upset her. Something he might have said or done.

Stepping under the spray, he closed his eyes and let the water run over him. A few seconds later, a small hand crept around his waist. Sucking in a breath, his stomach clenched at the feeling of her nipples pressing into his back. Whatever was bothering her obviously had nothing to do with the passion between them.

His questions would have to wait for now. He had more pressing matters to attend to.

Soap in hand, he turned her around so she lay against his chest. "Relax against me."

She complied, tilting her head back to lie on his shoulder. When his hands were full of lather, he swept them down her arms and placed her hands on his hips. "Keep these right here."

"Ash—"

"Trust me." It was half demand, half plea. In response, her fingers gripped his waist.

Smiling in satisfaction, he brought his own hands back up to her collarbone. In teasing strokes, he moved his fingers across her skin. Oblivious to the water spraying around them, his hands moved lower to gently cup her breasts. Their full weight filled his hands perfectly. God, he wanted this. He wanted her.

She shifted restlessly when he pulled lightly on her nipples. As he gently kneaded the smooth flesh, he could feel her fingers clenching and unclenching. Ash moved one of her hands up to cup his neck and took a moment to trace the curve of her side. The lather allowed his hand to guide easily over her wet skin, leaving small trail of suds in its wake. When he reached her hip, he used his knee to nudge her legs wider and slipped his hand between her thighs.

Maddie moved in a silent plea, but Ash was in no hurry.

One fingertip parted her wet curls, eliciting a soft moan of approval. With one arm now wrapped around her middle, he held her still against him, her back flush against his chest. He slid his arm up so it fit snug under her breasts, loving the feel of their weight on his arm. Loving how they bobbed gently with every move she made.

Her hips moved again, insistent this time. Chuckling softly in her ear, he whispered, "Slow down, love." She stilled, but he could feel her trembling in his arms.

With a light touch, he teased her clit. Maddie groaned in frustration as he continued to tease, never quite satisfying the hunger raging through her. It was sweet pressure, but not nearly enough. Moving her hips, she tried to get closer.

Ash used the opportunity to spread her folds and slide a finger inside. The hot water flowing around them was nothing compared to the wet heat around his finger. He had to grit his teeth to fight the delicious temptation of her ass rubbing against his straining erection.

Unable to help himself, he began to slowly slide his dick against the soft cleft of her ass. His finger moved in time with his shaft. As the water rained down, he slid effortlessly against her.

With his thumb still rubbing her clit, he used a bit more pressure and was rewarded with one of her breathy moans. How he loved the sound.

Plucking lightly, he manipulated the hardened nub as she began to move faster on his hand. Her motions increased the friction against his cock, forcing him to clench his teeth. Every second with her was the sweetest agony.

Rubbing harder now, he deftly brought her close to the edge. But before she tumbled over, he stopped. Silently she handed him a condom she'd placed on the edge of the shower stall. He was painfully grateful for her foresight. Otherwise he might not have been able to stop.

Turning her around, he lifted her against the tile wall. Her legs encircled his waist as he thrust inside. Her breasts were crushed to his chest as he pumped harder inside her. A few deep strokes and he was lost. An explosive climax gripped him as he poured himself into her. He barely heard her cry of release through the overwhelming pleasure.

Steam roiled around them as he helped her to stand on her own. Without words, Ash stood her under the spray and washed the soap from her body, careful not to abrade her hypersensitive skin. Stepping around the shower curtain, he tossed the condom into the wastebasket and returned to stand under the spray with her.

After they stepped from the shower some time later, each wore identical, satisfied smiles on their faces. While she rubbed a towel through her hair, he pulled on a pair of shorts. Moving so he was standing behind her, he brushed a brief kiss on the top of her shoulder.

She was looking at him in the vanity mirror. A small smile tugged at the corners of her mouth. "What was that for?"

The words *I love you* hovered on his lips, but he knew now was not the right time. So instead, he choked them back and forced a smile. "You're amazing."

Her cheeks flushed with pleasure at the compliment. In an effort to take the focus off her, she asked, "So, what are your plans for the day?"

"I'm going to be in the spa for a few hours."

"Really?" She sounded surprised. "Going to get all prettied up, are you?"

He gave her a playful tap on that delectable rear. "No. I'm going to go in a shaggy male and come out a well-groomed gentleman."

Sparkles of mirth danced in her hazel eyes. "Oh, I get it. That's a fancy way of saying you're going in to have a makeover without sounding like a wuss."

A smile threatened to curve his lips, but he needed to be able to maintain a shred of pride. "There's nothing wussy about getting a haircut and a shave."

"For a few hours?" Her eyebrows raised in disbelief. "What exactly are you planning on having them shave?"

"Just my face. They'll wax everything else." As he had hoped, her jaw dropped. When he was finally able to contain his laughter, he said, "They'll also put some gunk on my face, and I have to have some sort of wrap done. And trust me this isn't something I do on a regular basis. It was all part of the package deal I got with the room. I figured one time wouldn't affect my masculinity."

"Well, it wouldn't, but..." She tapped her chin thoughtfully. "You said you were getting a body wrap?"

Ash shrugged. "Something like that."

"If your masculinity can survive a former male underwear model spreading chocolate over you and then…removing it, I suppose you'll have a great time."

He grimaced at her teasing. "Don't worry. I made sure all my appointments were sans the erotica."

They shared a laugh at that.

"You were kidding about the waxing, weren't you?" Her voice held a thread of doubt.

He tugged on a strand of her hair. "Yes. I was kidding." He leaned closer so their foreheads were touching, a casually intimate gesture that didn't go unnoticed by either. "What are you going to do while I'm getting all prettied up?"

The green flecks in her eyes threatened to overwhelm the brown as she reacted to his nearness. "I'm going to be in the spa too. I'm getting a manicure and…" she trailed off as his lips claimed hers. Deliberately, he kept the kiss tender, keeping his desire under control. Instead, he allowed his deeper emotions to surface with a simple touch of his lips to hers.

Abruptly, she stepped back, breaking the contact. She tried to hide the trembling of her limbs as she gathered her clothes that had been scattered and left on the floor since Wednesday night.

But Ash saw. The woman who'd made love with him in the shower was gone, hidden behind whatever was bothering her. One minute she was a temptress, the next a reserved woman with shadows in her eyes.

Her composure obviously as brittle as the smile she directed at him moments later, she turned and didn't quite meet his gaze. "Okay then. I guess I'll see you later. I…um…" Shaking her head, she was unable to finish, and she slipped out the door as fast as she could.

Ash stood there for quite a while after she left, staring at the door she had all but run out of. A sigh of pure frustration crossed his lips.

Maddie was still running. She had to have read his intentions in that kiss and it had scared her. Now she was scared *and* running. Which wasn't good. What would it take to make her turn and run toward him instead of away?

Rolling his shoulders to ease the sudden tension, he turned back to the bed. A smile of remembrance flitted across his face. The passion she'd shared with him was more than simple lust. He'd bet his money on it. For the time being, he would let her run.

But he knew it. And she now knew it.

This had only been the beginning.

* * * * *

Maddie shut the door behind her and locked it. As if locking the bolt would hold the feelings at bay. Or hold Ash at bay.

"Get a grip, get a grip," she muttered.

That had been close. Much too close. For a split second, she had been tempted to say the words. Those three little words she wouldn't be able to take back.

She'd felt the words in his kiss. He'd let her feel the words, taste the words. He hadn't even needed to say them, because she knew. And when she'd understood, her arms had wanted to fling themselves around his neck and her mouth had wanted to open and declare the words as loudly as she could.

Thankfully, her sanity had returned in time. She'd managed to pull back and get control. Partial control, at least. Oh, who was she kidding? Where Ash was concerned, she had no control whatsoever. Not over her body, her mind or her heart.

Rubbing the heels of her hands against her eyes, she muttered once more, "Get a grip. I am not in l...love." Even saying the word aloud tripped her up. More forcefully, she repeated, "I am not in love."

But what else could describe this thing growing between them?

She had to believe that this whole thing was a little bit ridiculous. They'd only met a few days ago. At an erotic resort, no less. How in the world could she have developed feelings this fast? The rational side of her argued that it was impossible. Love at first sight was a myth as far as she was concerned. But a part of her wanted to be convinced of its existence.

"Arrgh!" Pacing back and forth in front of the sliding glass doors overlooking the garden, she tried to rationalize the situation out loud. "Okay, this is just a case of lust. Serious, animal lust. We have a chemistry that's great for the here and now, but it wouldn't make it through next week."

Not very convincing.

So she tried again. "On Saturday I'll be back home and he'll be back in Chicago. He probably won't even give me a second thought." The idea hurt more than she expected. But a gorgeous guy like Ash probably wouldn't even remember her name in a few months. Sad but true.

It was that particular insight that helped her to regain focus. She had another day of amazing sex to look forward to and then it was back to her normal life. This vacation was a once in a lifetime sort of thing and Ash was part and parcel of that scenario. If she'd learned nothing else this week it was that she needed to enjoy an opportunity like this while she could.

Looking around her room, she was temporarily at a loss. What was she supposed to be doing? Manicure and pedicure. Right.

They'd spent the last couple of days making love, sleeping, eating and making love again. Not necessarily in that order. She'd lost all track of time because of it.

Now it was Friday. The last day she would have to spend with Ash.

The thought caused her chest to tighten painfully. Barely swallowing the lump forming in her throat, she quickly changed her clothes and headed out the door.

Friday had to be one of the spa's busier days, Maddie realized, as she walked through the glass doors. Half a dozen people sat in the small waiting area, while a few others were being led back to rooms for their treatments. Maddie checked in and managed to grab an empty chair. Once again declining a drink, she rifled through a fashion magazine, not really seeing what was in front of her. Though she did check to make sure she was at least holding it right-side up.

Every few seconds she looked around, wondering if she'd see Ash. A part of her hoped to see him while another part dreaded it. She knew it would be better to have a little breathing room for a few hours. He was addictive to her system.

It was difficult to stifle the sigh that welled in her chest. There was nothing left to do but thoroughly enjoy this last day at the spa. And especially enjoy Ash. Reminding herself it wasn't every day a girl got to have a morning full of pampering and a night of unbelievable sex, she stood and smiled when she was called for her manicure. Her inner wild woman would have one more day to live it up before it was back to her normal life.

Chapter Fourteen

ဆ

At 3:30 in the afternoon, Ash made his way back to his room. It had taken a little longer at the spa than he'd originally thought. Anxious to get back to Maddie, he briefly wondered what sort of reception he'd receive. The way she'd run this morning made him wonder if she might even try to avoid him tonight. Not that he'd let her, of course.

Aloud, he said, "Guess there's only one way to find out." Stopping at her door first, he knocked.

The door opened to reveal Maddie in a short slinky robe belted loosely around her waist. Her smile was pure temptation as she opened the door wide enough for him to slip inside. "I was wondering when you'd be done."

Quickly sizing up the situation, he was heartened by the welcome in her eyes. Her smile said sex. He had a feeling whatever she wore under that robe—be it lingerie or her birthday suit—also meant sex. And the purr in her voice fairly dripped with sex. Hey, if it walked like a duck and sounded like a duck…

Ash was more than willing to allow her to play this role to the fullest. He was also more than willing to help her in any way he could. "Sweetheart, I came straight here."

"Good. Because I don't want to waste any more time." The flirtatious tone couldn't hide the sincere glint in her eyes.

Triumph welled through him as she pulled him closer for a kiss. Heart pounding with a mixture of needy desire and overwhelming love, he kissed her deeply, holding nothing back. This was what he'd been waiting for. She'd finally accepted what he'd known from the beginning. They belonged together.

She broke the kiss and stepped away. Reaching for her, he froze with his hand outstretched when she unbelted her robe and let it slide from her shoulders. Underneath she wore a black silk baby doll. The matching thong was the tiniest slip of material he'd ever seen. And definitely the sexiest.

He could feel desire heating his skin as she stood there. Pretty sure his heart had actually stopped beating for a few seconds, he could do no more than stare. With her hair unbound and her creamy skin wrapped in the luxurious silk, Ash knew without a doubt she was the most beautiful woman he had ever seen. He opened her mouth to tell her, but before the words could emerge, she covered his lips with her fingertip.

"No words. Tonight, I want to just enjoy each other. We don't need words to do that."

A protest formed in his throat, but he swallowed it down. She was right. They didn't need words to enjoy this night. He could show her how he felt, show her what she meant to him. Morning would be soon enough to tell her he loved her.

Smiling his agreement, he followed her to the bed.

After pulling his clothes off, she gently pushed Ash back onto the bed. He merely raised a brow and waited for her next move. Walking to the nightstand, she reached for the rest of the toys Kris had sent. Then she hesitated.

She examined the warming oil in her hand, then looked up at Ash. Her voice was quiet when she eventually said, "You know, I had planned to use some of these things to make tonight fun. But looking at it now, I realize all I want is you. I don't think we need anything else to set the mood." She smiled at his amused expression, but quickly sobered and repeated, "All I want tonight is you. And what you make me feel." The last was said so softly, Ash had to strain to hear her.

He had no time to wonder at her comment, because she straddled his stomach. Leaning forward, she kissed him. A deep, soulful kiss that went straight to his heart. And his dick.

He held her shoulders as she explored his mouth. Her tongue danced lightly around his own. Ash pulled the straps of her lingerie down just as she pulled his lower lip into her mouth. Baring her breasts, he filled his hands with her luscious flesh. Nipples hardened, she leaned into his caress, still loving his mouth. He gently rolled her nipples between his thumbs and fingers. Her whole body trembled with her need.

Her mouth moved to his ear, blowing gently. The simple, yet erotic act sent a shiver all the way down his body. He closed his eyes as she kissed his lobe. She'd found one of his favorite erogenous zones. Or maybe it was simply her. He pictured her even, white teeth as she bit gently on his ear.

While she was busy creating goose bumps along his skin, Ash skimmed his hands down her back and found the thong barely encasing her moist heat. Pushing the flimsy material aside, he delved between her folds, not surprised to find her more than ready for him.

Her mouth never leaving his skin, she grabbed his hands to hold him still. Scooting down his body, taking care to rub her breasts along his chest, she took his erection in her hands.

She hummed a sexy sound when she found a drop of arousal on the tip. He made a grab for her when she moved away. But it was only so she could shimmy out of her thong and the baby doll bunched around her waist. He lay back down when she again sat astride his thighs.

Carefully she moved up his body. Ash groaned as he felt the slightest brush of her curls against his shaft. Too far gone with desire, he couldn't even summon a smile at the ticklish sensation. Maddie caught and held his gaze as she took the bead of liquid off the tip of his dick with her finger and rubbed it against her clit. It was the most erotic sight Ash had ever witnessed.

As he watched, she spread his essence along her cleft, taking great care to lubricate her clit. His hungry gaze devoured her as she slid one of her small fingers inside her pussy. Ash watched her eyes close as an involuntary shudder coursed through her.

Christ, the image would be forever branded in his mind.

She slowly pulled her finger out and dragged it up to her clit again. Rapt fascination kept his eyes glued to her hand. He couldn't have looked away to save his life.

Maddie ruthlessly tormented him simply by touching herself. He watched her delicate fingers rub against her clit. Her faint moans of pleasure rolled over him as he watched a slight flush sweep across her skin.

When she pulled her hand away, Ash opened his mouth to object. She brought her finger to his lips to halt his words. He took the opportunity to draw her finger into his mouth. It was still wet with her arousal, and he let the flavor roll across his tongue.

All too soon, she pulled away. Leaning over his body, she lifted a condom off the nightstand. Staring into his eyes, Maddie painstakingly rolled the condom down his shaft. Ash let his hips lift at the teasing touch. She must have known he could take no more. Positioning her hips, she slid down onto his erection. The thin layer of latex did nothing to disguise the wet heat of her. Jaws tight with the effort it took to hold still, he let her rock against him. Every kiss, every caress nearly killed him.

It soon became too much and he rolled her beneath him. Intent upon giving her pleasure, he was oblivious to the urgency of her touch. He didn't stop to think about what it might mean. He didn't see the tears that clouded her eyes as she found her release. He held her to him after their desire was sated, not seeing the regret on her face. And he slept later that night, not feeling the wetness of her tears as they fell silently onto his chest.

* * * * *

It was still early enough in the morning that shadows filled the room. Staring down at him, Maddie could barely make out his features. Lying on his stomach, muscular limbs spread out over most of the bed, he looked even more delicious than the first time she'd seen him. She wanted nothing more than to crawl right back into bed, snuggle up to his warmth, and wake up when the sun was shining to make love again.

Instead, there she stood. Next to the bed, dressed and ready to leave. Her bags were packed. All that was left to do was checkout. She carefully placed the note she'd written on the pillow next to him, right where he'd be sure to see it.

It was time to go.

One last glance around the room assured her she'd not left anything behind. A bittersweet smile briefly turned her lips up. If only that were really true. No, she was certainly leaving something behind. And someone.

Squaring her shoulders, she resolutely walked away. From the man who would always hold her heart.

Chapter Fifteen

❧

The flight home had been a blur. Maddie moved through the baggage claim area in a listless fashion. A picture of her home swam into her mind, but rather than feeling eager to see it she felt a little depressed. Who wanted to open the door to nothing but empty rooms?

A happy voice intruded on her self-pity. "Maddie? Is that you?"

She turned her head and caught sight of a familiar blonde. Maddie was quickly enveloped in a warm hug from Kris. Her friend gave her no time to speak before she pushed her away for a quick once-over. "Oh my god! Hon, your hair looks great! I can't believe someone managed to talk you into this. Whoever the stylist was, they must have been something."

A vision of bright red hair came to mind, bringing a faint smile to Maddie's lips. "Yeah, you could say that."

Kris grabbed her hand. "And look at this! Your nails look great too. Heck, you're a total knockout. If you weren't my best friend, I'd hate your guts."

Maddie tried to summon a smile at the remark. The last thing she cared about at the moment was how she looked. She must not have been very convincing because the smile slowly faded from her friend's face.

"Do you forgive me?"

"You know, you were right all along. That vacation was exactly what I needed. So yes, all is forgiven. And thanks," Maddie added quietly.

Kris stared at her for a long minute, noting the pale cheeks and dark circles. Finally, she said, "No problem. Let's grab your luggage and get you home."

Grateful her friend hadn't asked questions in such a public place, Maddie took a deep breath.

She was okay. *Would* be okay. While they waited for her bags, Maddie tried to summon a hint of pleasure at being home. It really was good to see Kris. If anyone would be able to cheer her up, it was her friend. Maybe a girls' night out would help. Complete with gallons of ice cream and a funny movie.

If that didn't help, there was always work. Who knew what sort of catching up she'd have to do come Monday morning? It would probably be a good idea to go in a little early.

Grimacing at the thought, she tried again. Okay, it was always nice to be in her own home. Where there was never a shortage of ice cream. Neither was there anyone to prepare her the great food she'd become accustomed to over the last week. And sadly enough, she was going to miss her morning *Kama Sutra* tip.

On the other hand, she'd be able to sleep in her own bed. It always felt better to sleep in your own bed. Even if she was going to be sleeping alone. Swallowing against the sudden tightening in her throat, she gave up, willing her mind to go blank while trying to pay attention to the constant chatter from Kris.

After locating her bags, they headed to the car. Before leaving the airport parking lot, Kris turned to her. "I thought maybe we could grab lunch at the Italian place you love so much, but now I'm thinking takeout would be better. I have a feeling we have a lot to discuss."

"That would be great." A frown creased her brow. "But are you sure you don't have something else going on?" The frown turned into a teasing smile. "I mean, it is Saturday. I figured you'd have a date with some new hottie."

"Ha, ha. Unfortunately, my social calendar is depressingly empty at the moment. You're the only one who's been getting any action lately. So guess what? I get to live vicariously through you for the weekend. Because like it or not, you're going to spill all the wicked little details of your week in paradise."

Her good humor partially restored at their banter, Maddie replied, "Well, since I've had to live vicariously through your exploits the past couple of years, I suppose it's only fair I return the favor. Although I have to warn you I didn't do anything wild, like have sex in a restaurant bathroom or on a massage table in the spa. While there was another client waiting for a massage."

Kris waved her teasing away. "Oh please. Don't tell me that you wouldn't have done those things if you'd had the chance. And besides, that was a long time ago. I've matured beyond that."

Pretending to look thoughtful, Maddie tapped her finger against her chin. "Sure you have. It must have been someone else who was telling me only a few months ago they had sex on a golf course with a guy named Alexander something-or-other the third. And it couldn't have been you who, just a few weeks ago—"

"Okay, okay. I get your drift." Kris flashed an unrepentant grin. "So I like to have fun. What's wrong with enjoying sex?"

Laughing, Maddie just shook her head. "There's nothing wrong with it. Nothing at all."

"Exactly. Now, back to you. I want details about your week. In particular, I want to hear about all the men. Especially the one who has you down in the dumps. I'm thinking his level of sexpertise was so amazing, you didn't want to leave." That was the word Kris used to rate a man on his ability as a lover. It had never failed to amuse her.

Maddie didn't realize her voice had softened when she spoke. "He was absolutely amazing. The sex was incredible.

Earth-shattering. It wasn't just an orgasm. I felt it down to my soul, like I was—"

"Whoa, whoa, whoa. Wait a minute. When I said details, I didn't mean I wanted you to start spouting poetry and sappy stuff. I'm waiting to hear phrases like 'hung like a horse' and 'five times in one night'. Or even 'grunts like a wild boar'. You know, the really good stuff."

Maddie stared at her incredulously. "Grunts like a wild boar?"

Shrugging in an offhand manner, Kris admitted, "Hey, some guys do. You'd be surprised at some of the noises I've heard."

In shocked fascination, Maddie stared at her friend. Finally she found her voice, and was surprised to hear herself say, "Do you remember that guy I dated in college a few times? Trent? He squealed like a pig."

"I'm not really surprised. He looked like a squealer." Kris was nodding her head sagely.

"What?" Maddie snorted her disbelief. "How does a guy 'look' like a squealer? And why didn't you say something to me?"

"Hon, it's a gift I have. It's not something I can explain, I just know. Sometimes I can see it in their face, or hear it in their voice. I didn't say anything to you because I figured a little action would be good for you, squealer or not."

Maddie wasn't going to touch that one. In a choked voice, she managed to ask, "So can you tell with any guy?"

Kris looked thoughtful. "Most of the time. I can spot a squealer a mile away. The same goes for the grunters, cussers, moaners and yellers."

Laughing until tears streamed down her face, Maddie held her arms around her middle. "You are so full of it!"

"No, I'm serious. You would be wise to heed my words, grasshopper."

Maddie only laughed harder. Kris was so outrageous at times. After she was able to catch her breath, she looked over at Kris, who was smiling widely. Her friend always knew how to cheer her up. What would she do without Kris around to make her laugh?

She sobered quickly. The same thing she always did. Move on with her life. She was strong. She'd survive this. And if nothing else came of it, at least Kris would be able to steer her away from the squealers and the grunters.

The thought brought another peal of laughter from her lips. When Kris looked at her inquiringly, Maddie only shook her head, her mood lighter than it had been moments before. She only hoped it would stay that way.

Chapter Sixteen

ဆာ

Two weeks had passed since she'd walked away from Ash. Two of the longest, most lonely weeks of her life.

In order to keep her mind occupied, she'd thrown herself into working on the store. Instead she'd found herself thinking of Ash and reliving their time together. When it became obvious she was going to accomplish nothing, she'd put in more hours at work. When that hadn't worked, she'd gone out and bought a half-gallon of triple chocolate-fudge ice cream.

Triple chocolate-fudge couldn't do half as much damage as leaving Ash had. What were a few extra pounds compared to a broken heart?

Saturday afternoon found her on her sofa cradling a huge bowl of ice cream and an even bigger heartache. Gone were the cute and sexy outfits. In their place was a pair of faded navy sweatpants and an oversized white T-shirt. Her trendy new hairstyle was pulled back into a not-so-trendy ponytail. All of which did nothing to complement the dark circles under her eyes. Then again, she figured they helped to complete the whole heartbroken look.

As she sat there, contemplating whether or not to go ahead and lick the last bit of ice cream from her bowl, the doorbell rang, followed by a knock.

Without looking up, Maddie yelled, "Go away, Kris! How many times do I have to tell you I don't want to go?" Kris had been bugging her all week about getting out of the house.

When Kris had brought her home from the airport, it hadn't taken much prompting for Maddie to spill her guts. Three hours and several tears later she hadn't felt much better. Only weary to the bone. Kris had hugged her and then ruined the sympathetic gesture by saying, "Well hon, you walked away from something special that most of us will never have the chance to experience."

Kris had been right, but that didn't make it any easier for Maddie to deal with. So for her first week home, she'd refused to answer the phone or the door.

Never one to be deterred, Kris had simply cornered her at work. She thought Maddie was doing more harm than good by staying home alone. Actually, Kris had called it a "pathetic pity party of your own making". After hurling that unkind and untrue remark—never mind the empty ice cream cartons in the garbage—she'd then offered to take her out and help her get her mind off a certain sexy, dark-haired man.

It wasn't a pity party. Maddie preferred to think of it as a long period of introspection with a large dose of triple chocolate-fudge.

The knocking continued.

Climbing to her feet, Maddie walked to the door and yelled through the wood, "For the last time, no! I mean it! I don't want to go out. I don't want to have any one-night stands. And I certainly don't want you to find me a grunter to screw my brains out!"

Her irate tone must have worked, because Kris stopped knocking and the only thing Maddie could hear was silence.

Well, good.

Perfect.

That was exactly what she'd wanted. To be left alone with her heartache and memories. She resolutely grabbed her empty bowl and went to refill it, stopping when the knocking resumed.

"Oh, for the love of—" She flung the door open. Her angry retort died in her throat when she saw it wasn't Kris who stood on the threshold.

The silence stretched on for a long moment.

Speechless, she could only stare at the face she'd dreamed of for two weeks. Her eyes hungrily took in each detail. The dark hair that seemed a little longer and more disheveled, as if he'd repeatedly run his fingers through it. The rigidly held broad shoulders encased in a dark blue polo shirt that her fingers itched to touch. The firm lips that were pressed into a thin line. That gave her pause for a moment, but she bravely lifted her gaze to meet his.

"Hello, sweetheart." The deep voice she'd fallen in love with was now hard, edged with fury.

His gray eyes were burning, but this time it wasn't with the desire she'd become accustomed to. He radiated anger in tangible waves. And the only thing she could think about was the fact that he was here. With her.

"Ash." His name was a whisper on her lips.

In an almost violent motion, his hand slashed down, cutting off anything more she would have said. "No. Don't say a word. You never gave me the chance to speak before, but you're going to listen to me now." Without waiting for an invitation, he stormed inside.

Bemused and at the same time thrilled with his sudden appearance, Maddie could only stare. In the back of her mind she took note of the way his presence overwhelmed her small home. Wrapping her arms around her waist, she stood watching him pace her living room. The space seemed even smaller with him in it. At least it was no longer empty.

Minutes passed as he walked back and forth, his jaws clenched. Finally, he turned to face her. "You left me."

Maddie visibly flinched at the pain and confusion in his voice. The accusation hung in the air as they stared at one another. How could she respond to that? He was right. She had left him. At the time, she'd thought it was the right thing to do. Now she knew better.

Ash obviously didn't expect a response as he pulled a folded piece of paper from his pocket. Maddie immediately recognized it as the note she'd written. The well-worn creases in the paper told her he'd read it and reread it many times.

"Ash, let me explain."

As if she hadn't spoken, he began reading. "Dear Ash, I want to thank you for the most amazing week of my life. I came to the spa in order to get away and relax, never intending to meet a wonderful guy like you here. This week will always hold a special place in my memories. Best wishes, Maddie."

She'd written the note with good intentions, but hearing him read it made her realize how trite and impersonal it sounded. How horribly stupid and insensitive she'd been. "Ash, I didn't mean—"

"Didn't mean what? That I'm a 'wonderful guy' or that I'll always hold a 'special place in your memories'?" Or was it only the sex you'd remember?"

The harsh tone made her cringe and take an involuntary step back.

He advanced on her, clenching the note in his fist. "God, Maddie, I used to write more personal thank you notes to my Aunt Ellie when she sent me fruitcake for Christmas." He stopped directly in front of her. "I thought that you'd finally accepted it."

She knew what he meant, but the question tumbled from her lips anyway. "Accepted what?"

Instead of answering, he looked down at the note again. "That last night, you didn't want to talk. I should have realized it then, but I foolishly thought we could talk in the morning. When I woke up, the only thing waiting for me was this note."

The pain in his voice echoed in her heart. She'd been so selfish. It had never occurred to her walking away would hurt him too. She'd only thought of saving herself from bigger heartache. What a fool she'd been.

Wanting to hold him, she held back, knowing he wasn't quite through.

He looked directly at her then, holding nothing back in his gaze. "I let you run once. I'm not going to let you do it again."

Not daring to hope at his words, she held her breath.

"I've given you two weeks, sweetheart. Two weeks to figure out we were meant for each other. I know it's not a lot of time, but that's all you get." His voice was an anguished whisper when he said, "I can't wait for you anymore."

Dropping the note to the ground, he took hold of her hands. "When I decided to take a working vacation, I needed to get away from the life I'd created for myself. So there I was, sitting in a hot tub, wondering how I'd sunk low enough to find myself at an erotic resort *on a business trip*! It was apparent I needed to change something in my life. I was debating how to do just that, when the most beautiful woman I'd ever seen glides through the garden and into the water."

Maddie laughed softly through her tears. "I was gliding?"

He flashed her that gorgeous half smile she loved. "Considering the bikini you were wearing, you have to realize my attention was clearly not focused on your feet."

She flushed with pleasure.

"Maddie, I knew you were it for me. I saw you and immediately knew what I'd been missing in my life." He tenderly wiped away a tear that had fallen onto her cheek. "I want to spend the rest of my life with you. I want you for my wife, the mother of my children. I love you, sweetheart."

Stifling a sob, she threw her arms around his neck. Then just as quickly, she pulled away. "Ash, I'm sorry about the note. But I just didn't think it would work, and—"

He put a finger to her lips to silence her. "I know."

Maddie blinked in confusion. "You know?"

"Yeah. I, ah, talked with your friend Kris."

"You did what!?"

He shrugged his shoulders, unapologetic. "She called me this week and explained a few things."

Maddie considered that bit of information, wondering if she should be angry. Though at the moment, she was too thankful he was here. She smiled instead. "You know, we have her to thank for us meeting. She all but sent me to the spa at gunpoint."

"Hmmm, maybe we can send her there as a thank you." Ash nuzzled her neck, inhaling the scent that was uniquely her. A scent that had haunted his nights for the last two weeks.

Lifting his head, he looked at her in all seriousness. "I know you're busy trying to get your store up and running and I promise I won't get in the way of that. In fact, I was hoping you might want to take on a partner."

A small frown pulled at her lips. "What about the family business?"

Ash smiled. "When I explained to my dad I wanted to quit in order to marry the woman of my dreams, he was more than happy to find someone else to fill my position. Although one of the stipulations was that we have to give them at least two grandchildren. Soon."

"Only two?"

Laughing, he swung her around. "Sweetheart, we can have as many as you want."

"Mmm. Considering you have the stamina of a stallion, two shouldn't be too difficult to manage."

That comment earned her a light swat on the rear. Maddie could only laugh. Happier than she could ever remember being, she was sure her grin would leave permanent lines, it was so wide. Looking at the man who'd managed to turn her organized life upside down in a few short weeks, she had to say it out loud. "I love you."

* * * * *

Later that day, naked limbs entwined on her small bed, Ash lazily twirled a strand of her hair around her finger. "Sweetheart, something you said earlier is still bothering me."

"Hmmm?"

Because her head was on his chest, she missed the mischievous glint in his eyes. "Well, when I was knocking, you shouted something at me about not wanting to have a grunter screw your brains out or something like that."

Face flushed with embarrassment, she mumbled something into his chest.

"What was that?"

Sighing loudly, she turned to look at him. A brief explanation of Kris' "ability" had him howling with incredulous laughter. "I can't wait to meet her in person. What category do you think I fall under?"

Poking him in the side, Maddie grinned impishly. "Since you're a stallion, I suppose you would fall under the neighers." His pained groan sent her into a fit of giggles.

Snuggling up to him once more, she asked, "Were you serious about wanting to help me with the bookstore? It's so different from what you're used to."

"Now that you mention it, I've recently had an idea about designing apparel."

"Apparel? You're joking, right?"

Instead of answering her question, he replied, "You were actually the inspiration for my idea."

The doubtful look she shot him prompted him to say, "Sweetheart, let me tell you about a wonderful new invention for men. Never again will a guy be caught in an embarrassing situation with this strategically placed control panel..."

Why an electronic book?

We live in the Information Age—an exciting time in the history of human civilization, in which technology rules supreme and continues to progress in leaps and bounds every minute of every day. For a multitude of reasons, more and more avid literary fans are opting to purchase e-books instead of paper books. The question from those not yet initiated into the world of electronic reading is simply: *Why?*

1. ***Price.*** An electronic title at Ellora's Cave Publishing and Cerridwen Press runs anywhere from 40% to 75% less than the cover price of the exact same title in paperback format. Why? Basic mathematics and cost. It is less expensive to publish an e-book (no paper and printing, no warehousing and shipping) than it is to publish a paperback, so the savings are passed along to the consumer.

2. ***Space.*** Running out of room in your house for your books? That is one worry you will never have with electronic books. For a low one-time cost, you can purchase a handheld device specifically designed for e-reading. Many e-readers have large, convenient screens for viewing. Better yet, hundreds of titles can be stored within your new library—on a single microchip. There are a variety of e-readers from different manufacturers. You can also read e-books on your PC or laptop computer. (Please note that Ellora's

Cave does not endorse any specific brands. You can check our websites at www.ellorascave.com or www.cerridwenpress.com for information we make available to new consumers.)

3. *Mobility*. Because your new e-library consists of only a microchip within a small, easily transportable e-reader, your entire cache of books can be taken with you wherever you go.

4. ***Personal Viewing Preferences.*** Are the words you are currently reading too small? Too large? Too... ANNOYING? Paperback books cannot be modified according to personal preferences, but e-books can.

5. ***Instant Gratification.*** Is it the middle of the night and all the bookstores near you are closed? Are you tired of waiting days, sometimes weeks, for bookstores to ship the novels you bought? Ellora's Cave Publishing sells instantaneous downloads twenty-four hours a day, seven days a week, every day of the year. Our webstore is never closed. Our e-book delivery system is 100% automated, meaning your order is filled as soon as you pay for it.

Those are a few of the top reasons why electronic books are replacing paperbacks for many avid readers.

As always, Ellora's Cave and Cerridwen Press welcome your questions and comments. We invite you to email us at Comments@ellorascave.com or write to us directly at Ellora's Cave Publishing Inc., 1056 Home Avenue, Akron, OH 44310-3502.

THE
✝ ELLORA'S CAVE ✝
LIBRARY

Stay up to date with Ellora's Cave Titles in
Print with our Quarterly Catalog.

TO RECIEVE A CATALOG,
SEND AN EMAIL WITH YOUR NAME
AND MAILING ADDRESS TO:

CATALOG@ELLORASCAVE.COM

OR SEND A LETTER OR POSTCARD
WITH YOUR MAILING ADDRESS TO:

CATALOG REQUEST
C/O ELLORA'S CAVE PUBLISHING, INC.
1056 HOME AVENUE
AKRON, OHIO 44310-3502

erridwen, the Celtic Goddess of wisdom, was the muse who brought inspiration to story-tellers and those in the creative arts. Cerridwen Press encompasses the best and most innovative stories in all genres of today's fiction. Visit our site and discover the newest titles by talented authors who still get inspired - much like the ancient storytellers did, once upon a time.

Cerridwen Press

www.cerridwenpress.com

Discover for yourself why readers can't get enough of the multiple award-winning publisher

Ellora's Cave.

Whether you prefer e-books or paperbacks,

be sure to visit EC on the web at
www.ellorascave.com

for an erotic reading experience that will leave you breathless.